Elijah Newman Died Today

Elijah Newman Died Today

A Novella

Steven DeLay

RESOURCE *Publications* · Eugene, Oregon

ELIJAH NEWMAN DIED TODAY
A Novella

Resource Publications
An Imprint of Wipf and Stock Publishers
199 W. 8th Ave., Suite 3
Eugene, OR 97401

www.wipfandstock.com

PAPERBACK ISBN: 978-1-6667-5590-9
HARDCOVER ISBN: 978-1-6667-5591-6
EBOOK ISBN: 978-1-6667-5592-3

10/25/22

Once Again,
For Gabriella

Death is not too high a price for this—This taste of heaven.
—SCHILLER

A believer is a victor.
—ANTI-CLIMACUS

One

V ery soon, they would all be dead. This Elijah Newman knew. Or, at least, he had formed the judgment acknowledging so, even if their imminent deaths were a fate, which he himself had not yet internalized fully. He knew he too would die, although he knew it only in that uncanny way wherein knowing did not yet mean quite believing. Whether it was possible to wholly register such a belief was doubtful, it seemed to him. Of course, it was conceivable that some of the others had by now themselves done so, but there was no way for him to know whether anyone else had accomplished the feat. In any event, after having silently mulled the situation over as lucidly as he could, he had succeeded in more or less accepting the inevitability of his impending death, even if it were an increasingly proximate event that somehow still felt alien and distant. What struck him as especially odd, though, was the fact that, even without struggling to resist reconciling himself to the position in which he found himself, there was nevertheless a persisting sliver of hope, faint yet ineliminable, that his rapidly elapsing presence in this world might yet persist. He had to get home. This vague hope, for it was not an explicit wish, much less an overt prayer, that death would prove escapable, was swiftly transforming into a source of expanding guilt. That a deep portion of himself should unreflexively still feel as if death could be avoidable, and that the continuation of temporal existence was thus still to be desired, was a betrayal of hope, he realized. Were it neither to flag nor lose its dignity, hope must at this juncture turn its attention to what awaits on the other side of death, rather than continue to linger within the ordinary horizon sustained by the expectation of possible survival. To hope death could actually be averted felt petty, filthy even. In a crisis as desperate as this, one in which death was simply too certain to be denied, anything less than concentration on eternity would be indecently creaturely. Here and now, the previously banal everyday concern with time was no longer natural or reasonable. Here and now, time was at last irrelevant, for only the transcendent mattered.

Two

"Flight attendants, please prepare the cabin for emergency landing."

At once plaintive and measured, for a moment the tone suggested the voice of someone evidently impeccably resigned, but on the last word of the stated instruction when there occurred a slight crack, followed by a stifled sob, the pilot's primal fear revealed itself. When the flight intercom returned to silence, and there was only the sound of others weeping and wailing in the passenger cabin, it occurred to him how he had heard that in moments such as these, the whole of one's life might flash before one's eyes. Perhaps, then, he was merely an anomaly, but he did not find that to be the case. As it happened, he was in complete possession of his conscious faculties. His powers of thought, memory, and imagination were, so far as he could tell, as intact as ever. Had his entire life involuntarily begun flashing before his eyes, that may have in a way made things easier to bear. But here, even still, with the airplane plunging to the sea in what would be the final moments of their lives, the freedom of what to make of his time would be his, and solely his alone.

Three

O f Tolstoy, he had only ever read one of the author's later
works, a book on pacifism titled *The Kingdom of God is
Within You*. That in attempting to turn his thoughts to life, he
should find his mind had turned to literature instead was not so
unfitting. Contrary to what he knew devotees of postmodern art
maintained, art was mimetic, insofar as it emulated life, or at least
tried to express certain truths about it, truths which only art was
capable of expressing. At the very same time, life itself could be
equally mimetic. Just as art emulated life, so too life emulated
art. If, for example, he were to describe his present situation to
somebody on the ground, whomever he spoke to would invariably have equated the circumstances—careening down to earth in
a plane with only moments left to live—to Tolstoy's literary account of Ivan Ilyich. He had never read the story, but from what
he had read about it, his situation was reminiscent of Ilyich's own.
Ilyich was a man who lived his life as a social climber, ungrateful
for what was his, who comes to find that he had not lived a good
life, as he reflects on himself while dying alone in bed. He himself
had not been a social climber in life. But he was, like Ilyich, confronted with the fact of his impending death. Tolstoy's lesson for
the reader, it seemed, was that a life led without gratitude for the
gift of existence and compassion for others was empty and shallow,
and if one resented the indifference of others for not caring about
one's own suffering in the face of death, one must first determine
whether one's own life has been anything but self-interested. Ilyich,
apparently, was forced to endure the anguishing epiphany that his
life had been squandered purely on himself—there follows, he had
heard, some sort of deathbed conversion which transforms Ilyich,
reconciling him to both God and others. Had he read the story,

he would know the details, and he would have been able to see whether what Tolstoy had written about a man confronting his imminent death was accurate, whether the imaginative account of Ilyich was true to life, true to his own experience here, but that was not possible, having never read the Tolstoy.

If life were mimetic in that it could emulate art, there were further respects in which it was mimetic. For one thing, everyone in life emulated others. In the course of daily life, there had always been the constant pressure to conform, to please others, to be what others expected. Presumably, it was the spell of social conformism that had entranced Ilyich. And although he had not been wholly immune to feeling the pull of social norms himself, for a very long time, the majority of his adult life into young manhood, in fact, he had substantially freed himself from such expectations. He did not, then, have any profound regret about his life as a whole, as if he had lived it without ever being himself. There were, however, smaller episodic regrets. He felt called to take inventory of those, but before beginning to do so, he found himself studying those around him, to see how they appeared to be facing the situation themselves. This, as it happened, was another sense in which life was mimetic. Even here moments before dying, there was still an inherent curiosity with others, a curiosity in seeing how others were meeting the situation. That was a strange thing about death. In a way, there was a modicum of solace in knowing all the others were going to be dying, too. That there would be any comfort to take in such a fact was strange, of course, since it didn't at all alter the reality that he was going to die also. And yet, to be sure, there was some ineffable, unmistakable solidarity at work in knowing that each of them knew the others knew that they all were going to die, and that there was nothing any of them could do about it. Even though dying was the most isolating of all events, it for that very reason knit them together.

He looked out the window across the aisle. The angle of descent steepened, and they were now closer than ever to entering the cloud cover that had previously lied well-beneath the cruising altitude at which they'd been flying before the accident. The bottles and cups from the earlier meal service were rolling down the floor of the fuselage toward the first-class section. Moments before, the service cart had jostled loose, smashing against the cockpit door after barreling down the aisleway. More than a few of the overhead compartments had flung open, spilling luggage everywhere. As the cabin fell into disarray, everyone around him had put on the orange oxygen mask. There was no reason for doing so, however. At this relatively low of an altitude, there was already oxygen readily available naturally. He wondered whether others were continuing to wear the masks as a way of trying to deny that they were now closer to impact than ever, or whether perhaps they did so because they wanted to believe that somehow the crash was not imminent. It made for a pitiful scene, a cabin of ninety desperate individuals dutifully following social convention, even if they all must have known that going through the prescribed emergency procedures was effectively pointless. Whether one wore a mask or not was immaterial. Wearing a mask wasn't going to change anything. Nevertheless, the three female flight attendants had begun circulating through the cabin after the pilot's message, checking to ensure the passengers had secured their inflation vests properly. Some of the passengers, overcome with panic, had already inflated theirs prematurely. The flight attendants shuffled gingerly down the aisle together, grabbing onto the seats and armrests to keep their balance. Were he feeling sardonic, he could have laughed at the sight. Surely, everyone must know that the plane would simply disintegrate on impact. There would be no need to brave the water with a life-vest, because nobody would survive the crash. Reminding himself that he was short on time, he collected himself, turned his gaze from the window and his attention away from the others around him, and tried instead to decide which events from his past were worthy of memory.

Four

S mell, he knew it was said, was the sense most apt to evoke powerful emotions associated with the past. Olfactory memory did not so much produce a remembrance of what had been, it put one there again, in the flesh, as it were, as if the past were fully present, not as a past merely represented, but as a singular present undergone for the first and only time. Such memory could come close to enacting a repetition. Perhaps it was not surprising, then, that of all the things which could have conceivably come to mind, it was recollection of the smell of the eucalyptus trees that should saturate him now, transporting him to the seaside cove, where he would walk along the bluffs alone, contemplating what it meant to be anything at all. It was a place at which he had in time established a routine. He would drive out to the ocean on the single lane highway, alongside artichoke fields, the route nestled between rising oak hills in the distance, the wind blowing through the car's open windows, the sun shining in his eyes. He would clear his mind completely, trying to see the landscape for what it was, without any trace of himself, his thoughts, desires, memories, hopes, or fears intruding. Rendering himself translucent, he would almost disappear, a ghost hovering over the roadway, able to observe the surroundings, as if they had never been seen before, or would again. When his attention to the visible would wane, and his self-consciousness would restore itself, and so he would become an item of reflection for himself again, he would realize that if he were to die right there and then on the road by the sea, hardly anyone would notice. Even fewer would seriously care. It was not a despairing or self-pitying thought. The thought did not anguish him, nor did it offend any sense of pride he might have. It was instead merely uncanny, sublime even. Understanding fully that the world would go on as before when one was dead, as if one had never existed, was deeply humbling. To one moment feel as if one were everything and the world itself nothing, only then to feel as if the world were everything and oneself were nothing—it was an eerie phenomenon whose insight gave him to understand something universal and timeless about humanity. Like Hyperion, he felt it too. By the time he would drive down the oceanside switchback and park at the cove, he was so disassociated from the dance of life, that it almost was as if he were wholly anonymous, a purified consciousness without any semblance of worldly identity tethering him to civilization.

The squawking of the seagulls and crashing of the waves against the tidepools would intensify the anonymity. But every time, it was always that smell, the salt of the Pacific mingled with the eucalyptus groves atop the bluffs swaying beneath the cobalt sky, that would hollow him out from within, rendering him as if nothing, an invisible specter entirely at one with the wild being around him. He would remove his shoes and socks, roll up his jeans to his shins, and stand in the frigid shallows, gazing out to the horizon where the swirling white foam of the breakers met the gigantic, white puffy clouds puncturing the sky's blue expanse. Once his feet were too numb to feel, he would leave the water, sit down on the soggy sand, the coarseness of the pebbles against his palms reminding him that he was flesh and bone, and observe the gulls patrolling the shore for sandwich scraps or crumbs. Often, he would speak softly to the birds. And even though they did not reply by speaking, he felt that they at least listened. A deep rest-lessness would soon overtake him, and he would feel unable to sit where he was, so he would climb the dirt trail from the cove to the bluffs above. These solitary journeys to the sea, which he undertook years before he had yet met her, were times of great melancholy, even if he could not precisely identify what the source of its paradoxical sweetness was. Sitting up against the trunk of a tree beneath the canopy of shimmering leaves, facing the open sea, he was intensely aware of his finitude, more so than most others his age, he assumed, his sense of mortality making him question why he should even care at all about the future, as it was destined to fade away anyway. The immense beauty before him, he knew, one might well argue, should be an adequate consolation, since it was always possible to be grateful for the time one had to delight in all the seaside's splendor, but then again, it too would one day no longer be possible to experience. The roaring sea, the trees, the rocks, the sand, the birds—all would abide, long after he was gone. Death, it seemed, cast its pall over everything, for everything more persistent, more subsistent, than himself, was a somber reminder of his comparative insignificance.

Glancing again out the window across the aisle, and seeing they had now descended into the clouds, he yearned to be able to be on that beach once more, to be able to enjoy it justly, in a way his former ingratitude for creation would not this time spoil.

Five

*H**er*—it was imperative he give her thought in these remaining moments. He would never see her again, not in this life, he knew. That he was unable to tell her goodbye was agonizing, so much so that he chose to temporarily suppress the very thought of her entirely. But then, by striving to prevent the sight of her face from forming in his imagination, his consciousness consequently nearly succumbed to ushering back the fading retention of his recollection of the Pacific coastline, an expanse of former experience whose memorial presence had remained on the periphery of his conscious attention, never having faded away after having daydreamed about it momentarily previously. Hence, before noticing, he had nearly allowed an imagination of a future time at the cove to overtake him.

But, alas! There would never be such a time, it sunk in painfully, as the tender smell of the eucalyptus faded, and so with it the memory of the seashore, until he was planted firmly again here in his plane seat plummeting to this sea here below, the distant sound of that other sea he had used to view from the blufftops now nothing but a fading echo of what was about to become, or better, already was, an irretrievable past. Confined on the plane, somewhere over the turquoise waters of the Gulf of Mexico near, but not near enough, the shore of west Florida, things were more dire than ever.

The disarray, which had previously maintained itself within the bounds of the inanimate, had hungrily expanded its sphere of influence, the dissolution now eroding the social order among the living. To begin with, some of those who had already been inconsolable, and so had been crying loudly and uncontrollably, were now turning angry, evidently beside themselves over the fact that they were trapped, that there was no way out, and that death was insuperable. One woman, a middle-aged fiery redhead who was otherwise nondescript, had slapped her crying toddler brutally, and was now beating her fists violently against her catatonic husband's chest. A few rows in front of the disconsolate family, a young man in a tank top that had been meant to show off his tattoos, was screaming unintelligibly at the top of his lungs, gesturing threateningly toward anyone who so much as dared to glance at him. As for the flight attendants, they too had lost composure, and were no longer capable of doing what was necessary to carry on as if everything would be fine. They had not completed their check of the cabin to ensure passengers had secured their oxygen masks and life vests. One, the youngest among them, had simply collapsed in a heap in the aisle, from which nobody had bothered to retrieve her. By the looks of her crumpled mass, one might have thought she'd fainted, were her sobbing not evident in her heaving shoulders. The other two flight attendants had disappeared from sight, probably huddled together in the crew's service quarters, in which they could remain out of view from the passengers, whom they clearly no longer had any desire to assist or console.

Only heightening the mounting anarchy was the turbulence, which had struck suddenly when the plane entered the billowing thunderstorm clouds. The plane, which steadily had been gaining speed on its dive to the sea, and which already was causing everyone airsickness, was shaking violently from the rough air. More overhead containers sprung open, spewing luggage through the cabin, a pink roller bag striking a passenger in the head, and knocking him unconscious. The man's wife shook him desperately, trying to wake him. There was really no reason to attempt returning him to consciousness, if one thought about it, since in a couple of minutes he would be dead anyway. But the woman, who was beside herself with terror, could not tolerate the prospect of dying alone, so she continued to rub the unresponsive man's face and whisper in his ear, hoping to coax him back to presence.

The flitting recollection of his old pilgrimages to the eucalyptus sea cove had been pleasant, but allowing further memories of any type at all to occupy his attention was inappropriate, he felt. Memory at this point was distraction. Only prayer would do.

Six

" When I am afraid, I put my trust in you." Although summoning episodic memory to recall past events would be an unprofitable use of his time, the power of memory would here instead allow him to recall the words which he felt were most able to express what was in his heart. When the first engine had blown out, the plane twisting on its axis, he had experienced an involuntary, reflexive terror. The terror shortly thereafter receded into a mild dread, as he registered the fact that there was a serious malfunction with the plane. He was not in a window seat, so he could not see the wing, but he could see the trail of black smoke it was omitting, and which was blowing toward the rear of the craft where he was seated. Judging by the terrified faces of those in front of him who could see the damage, it had been urgent. The fasten seatbelt light had gone on. Then the cockpit intercom came on, there was the sound of frantic voices, the intercom went off, then it came on again.

"Ladies and gentlemen, please stay in your seats. We have just experienced a starboard engine failure. While we attempt to restore power, and figure out what's going on, stay calm, and keep your seat belts on. We will let you know when we have an update." The pilot didn't mention so, but the other engine was still fine. It would be necessary to land immediately, but the emergency was not evidently as cataclysmic as it had first seemed. It was only when the other engine on the port side failed as well, that he realized they were going to crash. What caused the engine failures was impossible to say. Investigators would study the black box data, and very likely determine what had gone wrong. But for everyone on the plane, it didn't matter. All that mattered was that it would no longer be possible to reach an airport on land. They would have to attempt a sea landing.

When the free-fall had begun, he had acclimated as best he could. The initial terror had dissipated. So, too, the dread. That he should address himself to God, by asking God to give him the strength not to fear, then, was not so much a desperate plea, for he did not feel any overpowering despair, but more so a request that God help him maintain his relative resignation. He recalled the disciples in their small boat on the sea of Galilee, overtaken by a violent storm, afraid they were to drown. They had run to the Lord sleeping tranquilly on a pillow, who awoke calmly, rebuked them for their faithlessness, and then commanded the storm to cease.

"Ask anything in my name, and I will do it," he called to mind. In principle, it was conceivable the crash could be averted. With God, nothing was impossible. Were he to pray for the engines, God could hear his prayer, restore them to flight, and save them all. They would not have to perish.

"Lord, please give everyone here peace. Let them put their trust in you. Ready us to meet you, if that is your will." He felt sorrow for those around him who, for whatever reason, had not yet come to terms with the situation, and where clearly terrified of dying. He assumed that, whether they themselves realized so, they must not yet have made peace with God. They were unready to die. If he felt ready, he should focus on doing what he could to help others be the same.

"Lord, your will be done. If you wish to spare us, thank you. Thank you. If we die here, show us your mercy. Show us your love. Let us be in your kingdom." He turned to the woman sitting in the middle seat, locked eyes with her, and smiled gently. Tears were coming down her cheeks. She removed her glasses, wiped them against her shirt, dried her tears, blew her nose with a napkin, and put on her glasses.

"It'll be okay," he said to her over the noise of the surrounding tumult.

The woman winced, apparently offended, or at least unconvinced, by his words. She was someone whom in daily life had scoffed at the notion that God took any interest in human events. Yet now, facing death, the fright she was experiencing had deprived her of breath, and she was unable to say what she was thinking. Part of her, it appeared, wanted to believe there was a God, and that a miracle was possible. He could see she did not know where to begin sorting out her life before God, that she had lived away from God for so long, that she did not know how to reconnect with him after such a long estrangement.

"I hope so," she said distantly, burying her face in her palms. A brief silence ensued. "I wasted my whole life," she said in the tone of a confession.

"It's okay," he said again.

"No, no, no—no, it isn't," she said self-accusatorily, beginning to sob. "I'm sorry for everything," she said quietly, this time mostly to herself.

The woman, like Ilyich, was evidently haunted by the realization her entire life had been a lie. He wanted to say there was still time for her to overcome regret and affirm life, by reconciling herself to God, but he worried that his saying so, which would have been motivated by kindness, might be misinterpreted for something else, and she would merely become angry with him. Perhaps it was selfish of him, but he decided to remain silent.

The man in the window seat, who till then had said nothing, turned to them both. "Maybe there will be a miracle," the man said.

"A miracle? Hah!" the woman snorted.

"Why not? Maybe if you prayed, we'd get out of this," the man countered.

"Oh, so it's my fault now? I won't pray to some stupid God, who is letting this all happen anyway, so now I'm responsible that we're all going to die? Or I guess God is just punishing us all for how he made us, right? Woe is me, a sinner. Boy, that one makes sense," she laughed contemptuously. Elijah saw the woman in the middle was laboring under a false conception of God. Most likely, she had only the vaguest grasp of the historical and theological origin of the conception. But Elijah recognized it well. It was the arbitrary, vengeful God of Calvin's predestination—the *Deus absconditus*.

"Got any better ideas, lady? Newsflash: the pilot's barely keeping this thing gliding, we're losing altitude real fast, and we're all gonna be hitting that water real fast, real soon," the man continued.

The woman snorted. "Yes, thank you very much, Mr. Newsman. I am aware. God, you are stupid," she said.

The man looked to Elijah. "You taking her side?"

"I believe it is good to pray. I was praying myself," Elijah said.

"See! There you go. This guy knows. Maybe God will let us out of this one," the man said, peering out the window, though hardly anything was visible through the smoke from the engine.

"Well, I'm very glad that you two have bonded over your disagreement with me. Glad to be of help," the woman said sarcastically. "Ugh, men," she said. She buried her head in her hands, and went back to crying.

"Hey, why don't you have your jacket on?" the man asked Elijah. Knowing that if it really came to it, a life-vest would prove useless, as nobody would survive the impact, he had decided not to bother putting one on. He was about to explain himself, but before he did, the woman interjected.

"You idiot. Why do you think? We're all going to die anyway. You're not going to be alive to need the vest after this thing slams into the water," she said.

"Well, why then do you have yours on?" the man asked. The answer, of course, was that everyone had simply put one on when one was supposed to, and so the woman had decided that she may as well do so also. It had been an especially absurd instance of everyday conformism.

Nearer to the moment when it would be time to brace for impact, he left the two others to bickering, and returned his attention to God.

Seven

"The end of the just," a verse somewhere in Wisdom said, "is blessed." He believed he was just, though he had not always been so. There had been the indiscretions of youth. But he had changed his ways eventually, and gone on to live a life free of the sins that had formerly plagued him. He was not perfect, in that it was always possible to increase in holiness, but his heart, so he thought, was certainly in covenant with God. He loved the Lord. Assuming, then, that he was indeed just, it followed that his end here, death by plane crash, must somehow be blessed.

There were many reasons someone might adduce for concluding so were preposterous. To begin with, one might think it was stretching credulity to view death, in any circumstances, even the most fortuitous, as a blessing. If life was an inherent good, its deprivation would appear to be an evil. This appeared to be borne out by the fact that even those who claimed not to have a desire for immortality would always choose more life over immediate death, if presented the choice. And yet, from this it in no way followed that everyone wanted to live forever. It was a paradox, to be sure, but someone had once explained the puzzle. Suppose each day one were offered the choice of whether this would be one's last day, or whether one would like to have tomorrow as well. Every time that one was posed this option, one might well say, "No, I don't want today to be my last; I want to live tomorrow too." Yet, from the fact that each time one was asked this, one would request another day of life, it did not logically follow that one wanted to live forever. It seemed this implied that death was simultaneously both good and bad, which was a contradiction, that death was something one would never embrace in the immediate, since more life always seemed preferable, but which, at least in the abstract, could be affirmed, insofar as one did not want to live forever, to be immortal, either. Of course, there was always the possibility that whoever had concocted the thought-experiment was simply self-deceived, or lying. Perhaps everybody deep down really did desire immortality, whether he admitted it or not.

He mouthed the other words from that same stretch of text, words that spoke to him, and gave him comfort, "God made man to be immortal, to be an image of his eternity."

On the plane, it was palpable nobody aboard wanted to crash. There were only varying degrees to which everyone was resigning himself to the unwelcome fact that they would. If he had more time, he would have pondered the paradox of the immortality thought-experiment further, attempting to reason his way to a resolution. But that sort of thinking didn't matter anymore, if it ever had. Better simply to accept that death as such, even here and now, was a blessing for him owing to the grace of God, and proceed from there.

Eight

"Lord God, thank you for your mercy. Thank you for your forgiveness. Thank you for saving me from death. I love you. I need you now. Please be with me. Don't forsake us." These words of his heart, were anyone able to have heard, surely would have been cause for confusion. Elijah Newman was about to die, and yet he was grateful to God for having saved him from death. On its face, there was a contradiction. But it was only an apparent contradiction. What he meant was not that God would spare him from bodily demise. He meant, rather, that God had redeemed his soul, had saved him from spiritual death, from eternal separation from God.

As he well knew, death was a term designating a multiplicity of things in the Scriptures. In the first place, there was a kind of living death. This was the state, truth be told, in which most of the others on the plane, the woman next to him included, were languishing. They did not know God. As their visceral aversion to death revealed, it was possible to be dead while still alive. This was the condition one found oneself in when one had not been redeemed from the sting of death, because one did not yet possess the hope of eternal life. To live life apart from God in this fashion, unredeemed in one's sin, was thus to be already dead despite still living. Or, more exactly, to be dead while alive, to not know God, was to be in despair over knowing that one could not die. For, the one dead in sin wanted to believe death would be the end—that one was not immortal, that there would be no judgment. It was only when the prospect of demise suddenly came upon one, then, that one realized one had already been living as dead the entire time. Typically, that one was dying by not living in Christ could go undetected. The world and its diversions and distractions enabled this easily. To be in covenant with God, to have the hope of eternal life, in contrast, was to have overcome death, such that one would in that respect never die. One remained as mortal as ever, in that one's temporal existence in the world would still at a point come to an end. Spiritually speaking, however, if one had Christ, then one would never die, because one would live in him after leaving the world. Christ had risen from the grave to defeat death, to vanquish the human fear of it, he thought. To thank God for saving him from death, then, meant gratitude that even as he was about to meet his demise, he could look to the hope of eternal life, which had negated what the world considered to be the finality of death. This made affirming his looming demise without regret possible, for he was grateful for the time that had been his, and although more time would be wonderful, were God to bestow it, he was calm, accepting that death would in any event not be the end, but rather a passage to eternal life.

"He that hath the Son hath life."

Buoyed by overwhelming gratitude, his heart felt clean and pure, open to God, from whom he had nothing to withhold or conceal. When his consciousness began drifting back to thought of her, this time he did not feel any need to stymie it, by directing his attention to something else. No, it would be very good to think on her, to think about how much he loved her. After all, that she was his love, that he had known her for the time that had been theirs, was itself a gift from God.

On nights like the one about to fall, he would lie still in bed next to her, listening to the patter of the summer rain against the bedroom window. They would be watching a movie, or talking about some detail of the day, when she would quickly drift off to sleep, as was her habit, and he would be left alone on what would be a night vigil. He would rub the cat's chin, who was nestled between them, and study the droplets forming a beautiful fractal on the glass. The orange streetlight from the lamppost would coruscate through the rain beads, creating a neon spectacle as brilliant as it was serene. Sometimes, he would simply enjoy the silence, other times, he would put music on the record player, the sound of oldies from the forties or fifties permeating the room. She would tell him how she liked that, liked knowing that he was still wide awake next to her, keeping watch after she had receded into dreams. He would listen to her light breathing, stroke her hair, and think about the children they did not yet have, but one day would.

The subject of names would frequently recur.

"Okay, what about for a boy? What do you like?" she would ask.

"You know I would prefer something biblical. Something handsome but strong. A friend of mine once pointed that out to me. Strong male names have only one or two syllables."

"Which one?"

"How about Luke?"

"Luke is good. How about Jude? I've always liked Jude."

"I used to not like it. But since you've mentioned it before, I thought more about it. I like it now. That could work. How about Samuel?"

"Samuel is good. I like Sam."

"Most of the Sams I've known have been good."

"Me too," she would say.

"Girls?" he would ask.

"I don't like Mary or Ruth or anything like that. Boring. Maybe Vivian. Or Emma. I really like Isabella."

"Another Ella?" he would laugh.

"How about Elijah Junior for a boy, then?"

"No way. I think it's so narcissistic when a man gives his son the same name. I'd never do that. How about Enoch? Same motif behind Elijah," he offered.

"Enoch?" She got a scrunchy look on her face. "Sorry," she said.

"All right. Enoch too odd? How about Polycarp then?" he said kiddingly.

She laughed.

"Okay, so Enoch's out. Jude is good," he said.

Nine

As he began to mull over that he would never be a father, something extraordinary happened. The intercom had come on again.

"Ladies and gentlemen, I, uh, I, well, I don't know what to say. The port engine has just now come back. I'm not sure why it went out to begin with, but my goodness, the main thing is that it's back. We're too far out to turn around and reach Sarasota, so we're going to press on and land in Tallahassee, which is the closest airport. Stay seated with your seatbelts on, and please don't remove your life jackets." It occurred to him that fuel may be an issue, but given the fact that the pilot didn't mention it and sounded relieved, it was safe to assume that would not present a problem.

Everyone in the cabin felt the plane beginning to level off. They were not yet climbing, but neither were they falling.

"It's a miracle! Haha! I told you!" the man at the window proclaimed.

The cabin erupted in cheers and whistles. People were hugging one another and high-fiving. There were tears, but now of joy. The woman in the middle hugged the man at the window. "I can't believe it! If you want to call it a miracle, that's fine. It doesn't matter. We're alive!" she exclaimed. The two embraced.

The man looked at him, "Thank you for your prayers, buddy!"

He was about to tell the man that he had nothing to do with it, since he'd failed to pray for the plane not to crash. The engine coming back on was purely God's will. He opened his mouth, but before the words came out, he heard groaning. The flight attendant who had collapsed in the aisle was lying sprawled out on the floor. In the euphoria, nobody had noticed. He sprung up from his seat and walked over to the woman, tapping her on her shoulder.

"Miss, are you okay? Let me help you up." The woman flopped over on her back and slowly opened her eyes. "Where am I? Are we—"

"We're on the plane. The engine came back on. The pilots are taking us to Tallahassee. C'mon, let me help you up." Another man came over also, and the two of them together lifted the woman to her feet.

"Thank you. I should get back to work," she said, adjusting the name badge on her uniform. The other man handed the attendant her hat.

When Elijah took his seat, the two flight attendants who had disappeared were moving about the cabin again. "Ladies and gentlemen, please stay seated. Keep your seat belts on. The pilot has indicated that you must remain in your life jackets, too. Please wait for further instructions," one of them said over the intercom from the first-class cabin.

"Sir, it was very kind of you to assist our colleague. But in the future, please stay seated, and let us take care of it. Your safety is our first priority," the other flight attendant said. He almost pointed out that she and the other attendant had left their colleague on the floor, and that they had abandoned their duties when things had seemed hopeless, but he thought better of it. There was no reason to spoil the jubilation, and if those who should be embarrassed for their actions wanted to pretend that nothing had happened, that was to be expected. With the emergency averted, the everyday social norms that had been evaporating during the emergency were again relevant. People would be willing to say and do the absurd.

"Oh, also, if you would, please put on your life jacket. Pilot's orders," the woman said, as she moved down the aisle to check in on others.

The pilot came on the intercom again.

"Flight attendants, thank you for your composure. We are all lucky to have you aboard, I'm sure the passengers will agree." There was raucous applause. "I think what we've all just been through calls for a celebration. If you would, please break out the champagne for everyone, and I'll see you all on the ground. I'll have further details as we enter our approach to Tallahassee." There was more cheering, this time even louder than before.

An older man sitting on the boundary between the main cabin and first-class stood. He removed his cowboy hat solemnly, and waited for everyone to quiet. When he knew he had everyone's attention, he spoke, his thick Texas drawl booming through the plane.

"I don't know about y'all, but I sure was praying there. I think we should all take a moment of silence to thank the Almighty." A few of the passengers sighed or rolled their eyes, but the majority of the plane seemed agreed that it was only fitting to take a moment to acknowledge the miracle. There were a few seconds of silence.

"Yee-hah! We made it!" the cowboy exclaimed. "Let's drink that champagne, and enjoy the fact that we'll be feet on the ground soon. I ain't ever flying again!" The cabin burst into laughter and more cheers. It was uncanny, Elijah thought. Everyone was justifiably ecstatic to be alive, and yet, that they were all going to die one day, anyway, had not changed. They were still mortal. Death remained as certain and inevitable as it had been moments ago. And yet, it had vanished, reduced to nearly nothing—nothing but a pure phantom.

The flight attendant walked over to the man, and with a playful smile on her face reminded him that everyone must stay seated for the remaining duration of the flight. He tipped his hat to whistles and further applause, then sat down.

Ten

T o be sure, he was elated. That they would be on the ground, safely, meant that soon he would see her again. He had desperately wanted to be able to hold her hand when he thought that he never would be able to do so again. Now he would. If moments ago he had felt that thinking about his earthly life was no longer pertinent, for it had been time to ready for eternity, he felt it was now permissible to think about all the gifts which were to be his again. To begin with, it was no longer necessary only to reminisce about cherished times they had shared before. There would be new ones to forge.

His imagination assembled images of the coast of Sardinia, ancient cliff faces towering above a majestic secluded cove, the thin edge line of white sands holding firmly against the tide of crystalline sapphire sea. They had talked often about visiting the place, but never done so. He had always thought they would, and now they could.

Instead of Europe, they had for some time made Florida their leisure destination. There was an irony in this, she had noted, because he had for the longest time before visiting stated that he had no interest in ever going. There had been a certain loyalty he had felt to the Pacific, even if he had to concede the Gulf and Atlantic were much more hospitable to swimming. Their first time to the sunshine state had changed that forever. The Pacific was scenic, and its views were stunning. But there was simply nothing better, he had come to find, than floating in the warm waters of the Gulf, taking in a sunset beneath the palms, the tropical breeze impressing the glory of existence upon his skin. Although places such as Key West were more famous, their favorite spot, Anna Lucia, was a small island town on the western coast of Florida. He had ended up here on the plane, because he'd taken a trip there alone scouting for possible rentals, maybe even a house to buy. They had wanted to go together, but she couldn't take off time from work. He laughed softly when he recalled what she had said at the airport when dropping him off.

"Be careful for sharks."

"It'll be fine! I'm probably statistically more likely to die in a plane crash."

"You know I wish I could go with you, so we could be together. I hate when you fly alone."

"If anything happened, I wouldn't want you there. Better for me to die first."

"Yeah, good point," she said laughing. "I'm kidding."

"You'd be okay. If something ever happens to me, don't feel guilty."

"Don't say that. Text me when you land," she had said. "You know, if I died first, you'd be fine. I bet you would be married to someone else within six months."

"No way. I would never remarry. It would be a bachelor life for me."

She laughed. "I don't think so. You totally would find someone else."

"Why do you think that?" he asked.

"It's not a bad thing. It's just how you are. Remember the neighbor from your old apartment? Boy, she sure loved you. I bet you could marry her," Ella said.

"I don't want to marry anyone else," he said.

"Remember, let me know when you've landed. I always worry," she said.

His mind turned to another moment from years ago. At the time, they had been dating for a few months, when Ella had said she wanted to take a break. She had said it wasn't his fault, that she needed space to think. She never said why, and he never asked, but he suspected that she was torn, and that she probably had started seeing an old boyfriend of hers. Not long into the break, he had encountered the neighbor from downstairs, a mousey art school type. When he opened his mailbox on the first floor, he turned around to find her opening her door to leave for work.

"Oh, hi," she said.

"Hi."

There was a pause. She seemed nervous.

"I see you around here a lot, but we've never properly introduced ourselves. You live upstairs?" she asked.

"Yeah, been here a few months now. You?"

She locked her door, then leaned against the wall nonchalantly. "Couple years. I always tell myself I should move, but I never do." The way she said it suggested that she was glad she hadn't moved, since now she'd met him.

"Yeah, it's easy to get stuck in a routine."

She studied him pensively. She was about to speak, but she paused again. Then she spoke, "You know, you seem like you're sad. In pain."

"Oh," he said. He didn't want to discuss Ella with her.

"I know how it feels."

"What?"

"Break-ups. I had a boyfriend." He waited for her to continue. "We were together for a long time. But there was a problem. Do you know what DID is?"

"Disassociative identity disorder?"

"Yeah. Most people haven't heard of it. If you're familiar with it, it'll be easier to explain what happened."

"Okay."

"Well, it's kind of like dating someone with dementia. They have these blank spells for hours, sometimes even days. They don't remember who they are. We would be sitting on the couch, and he'd leave to get something from the grocery store or whatever, and he'd disappear for hours. He wouldn't remember me, or know he was with me. Or, we'd make plans to meet, and he'd never show up, and I wouldn't hear from him. At first, I thought he was seeing someone else. But later I learned about the condition."

"What was causing it?"

She sighed. "That's the thing. He never said. I don't think he really knew. I always felt like it was something terrible from the past, but whatever it was, he had repressed it."

"So, what happened?"

"I hung on for as long as I could."

"Then you broke up with him finally?"

She laughed. "No. Actually, one day he just left, and I never heard from him again. He disappeared."

"I'm sorry."

"It's okay. There's loving someone and then there's loving the idea of them. Being with him taught me the difference."

"I think I see what you're getting at," he said.

"Most people want you to love an idea of them. If you love them for who they really are, they can't take it. They don't like themselves, and your love only reminds them of it, so eventually they push you away." She glanced away awkwardly, as if she had said too much. She wanted to invite him in, but he could see her change her mind. She waited to see whether he would suggest they get a coffee or see a movie. When he didn't offer a date, she waited for him to say something else instead.

"Wow, I'm not sure why I told you all that," she said.

"It's fine. I should be going," he said.

"Me too. I'm Falyn by the way."

"Elijah." He paused a moment thinking. "Wait," he said. "I know what it is. This may sound odd, but I think your voice sounds familiar."

She blushed. "From the radio?"

"Yeah, that's it."

"Guilty as charged. I'm the one, DJ Slug Smooch. You listen to the station?"

"Back when I was in college, some of my friends used to work there at the station. Every once and a while, I'll still turn it on to see what's playing. I must have heard your program at some point."

She smiled expectantly. "I'll talk to you later. Bye," she said.

It was the one and only time they talked. Shortly afterwards, he heard from Ella, and it wasn't before long that they were back together and married.

At the airport in Florida, he had ignored the taxis. A local, whom they had met on a previous trip, was there to pick him up. "Elijah, good to see you," the man said affably. The man removed his sunglasses, rubbed his hand through his grey hair, and extended his palm to shake hands.

"Bob, good to see you," Elijah said.

"Just you this time?"

"Yeah, Ella's stuck at work. I won't be here long. Just a few days. I'm scouting out places for us. We may be moving down."

"Ah! Our new neighbors! I'll have to tell Clara. Well, it'll be good to have you at the rental for a few days. You'll see we've put in a lot of work. I'm glad your flight arrived on time. We have to hurry. Bingo night tonight. The pot's over three thousand! Wanna play?"

"Oh, no. You have fun. I'm gonna take a stroll, maybe go for a swim. Nothing crazy," he laughed. When they pulled up to the yellow cottage, he thanked Bob for the lift, set his things down inside, and texted Ella. "Made it. Bob and Clara say hi. I'm going to take a dip, then find dinner. Love you."

Outside, Bob was trimming a yellow rose bush before leaving for bingo.

"You know, this is the best time for a swim. The tourists all make the mistake of hitting the beach in the morning. They suffer through the noon sun, and by early afternoon, they're fried. You show up late in the afternoon like this, and the water's been heated by the sun, but the wind's picked up a bit, and it's bearable to be on the sand."

"That's what I tell Ella!"

"You're a natural," the man laughed. "Hey, by the way, you ever try the water bottle trick?" The island had a large manatee population, the gentle beasts congregating on the beach by the jetty, opening to the marsh. Bob had once mentioned that if one took a water bottle, the manatees would sometimes drink from it.

"Ah! Thank you. I'll have to bring one. We've done the lettuce thing, though." Due to all the pesticide runoff from the nearby golf courses, the sea algae were in decline. As a result, the manatees were facing starvation. When Ella heard about it, she immediately had wanted to feed them all. "I bet they'd eat lettuce," she had suggested. Every time they had since visited, they would buy lettuce heads from the grocery store, walk out to the jetty, and feed the hungry manatees.

He strolled to the beach, entered through the picket fence next to the familiar mangroves, set out a towel, took off his shirt, applied some sunscreen, and stepped into the clear water. A solitary heron stood on the shore, looking on. That afternoon, while floating effortlessly in the placid sea beneath the setting sun, the cypress trees back ashore swaying in the wind, he realized he was experiencing the closest thing to eternity this life had to offer.

Here on the plane, he watched everyone around him sluff off the remembrance of death. The crash averted, they thought they were alive, which for them really only meant a return to the living dead. Lest he forget God also, it occurred to him that he should continue praying. Had he been the superstitious type, he would have taken the vague feeling of unease forming within him as a premonition, but he chose instead to banish it from his mind.

"Champagne, sir?" the flight attendant asked.

"Oh, no. No, thank you. I'm fine." The woman appeared surprised, but said nothing. "How about you two?"

"Of course! Fill me up," the man at the window said.

"Please!" the woman in the middle said. The attendant poured the champagne, and the man and woman clinked glasses. "Cheers to what will be an amazing story!" the woman said.

"I wonder if the news will cover this," the man said. The man paused and glanced over. "Boy, not to be mean or anything, but you're a real killjoy, buddy. You look like we already died," the man laughed.

"Religious types," the woman sighed. She finished chewing a chocolate, then cleared her throat. "Always thinking about something imaginary, rather than reality." It was a comment the woman would never ordinarily have made to a stranger, but the fact that they all felt a residual bond of intimacy from having undergone a near-death experience together, combined with the fact that the usual social norms of daily life had not yet quite solidified fully, led her to let slip what was really on her mind. For a moment, she thought to apologize, but when Elijah didn't say anything, she and the man at the window decided to forget about the faux-pax, and focus instead on the champagne.

"Champagne is great, but a snack would be nice," the man at the window said. When the woman in the middle didn't offer him a chocolate, he frowned, and said, "You're lucky to even get a bag of pretzels on a flight these days."

"Perhaps you should just be grateful," the woman said. It was true, but the fact that she said it so nastily suggested that she could do well to take her own advice. The man almost said so, but bit his tongue.

"Excuse me! Flight attendant," the woman said.

"Yes?"

"Sorry, but may I have a refill?"

The flight attendant shook her head no. "I'm sorry ma'am, but refills aren't possible. We have to ensure there's enough champagne for others." The woman in the middle was about to protest. But the coy smile forming on the face of the man at the window, who was about to pounce on her hypocrisy if she complained, ultimately dissuaded her from saying anything.

Elijah reached beneath the seat in front of him, retrieved his Bible from his bag, and opened up to read whatever verse he would find underlined on the page.

Eleven

With the champagne having begun taking effect, heightening the original euphoria everyone felt at their good fortune to be alive, it understandably took everyone a moment longer than it otherwise would have taken, in order to comprehend what they were being told. For a moment, there were some who thought they were the victims of the world's cruelest practical joke. When they realized the voice over the intercom was serious, the old familiar fear returned.

"Flight attendants, secure the cabin immediately. We have an emergency. The port engine has failed again. Tallahassee was close, but a water landing may be inevitable," the pilot said. That the pilot spoke of land in the past tense was suggestive. They would not make it.

Immediately, there were screams of grief and disbelief, curses and mumblings. Within a few more seconds, the weeping and wailing began again in earnest. When the engines had failed the last time, there had been shock and fear. This time, there were both as before, but also an overwhelming undercurrent of rage. People, Elijah saw, felt like they were being cheated. God, they clearly thought, was toying with them.

"Oh, my God," the woman in the middle hissed. "Boy, why doesn't that idiot in the cowboy hat stand up now?" She started sobbing. The man in the window seat, who looked crestfallen, was waiting for her to say something snide to him directly, but she was so overcome with grief and fear, that she was solipsistic, oblivious to everyone and everything around her. The young tattooed man, who was already drunk, threw his champagne against the cabin wall in disgust. "Well, I guess we're all going to die, after all," he said despondently. The flight attendants, who had been enjoying the adulation they were receiving from the passengers in the wake of the short-lived miracle, stood frozen in disbelief, unable to say or do anything. As the plane began again plunging to sea, nobody said a word about the oxygen masks or life vests. He hadn't bothered to put his on before, and wouldn't this time, either.

Twelve

A fter having flown above the clouds only to descend into them
once again, the turbulence had returned, along with the airsickness. He felt he would vomit. Despite the physical discomfort,
he did his best to concentrate on what was on the page.

> Are not two sparrows sold for a farthing? And one of
> them shall not fall on the ground without your Father
> knowing it.

These words, which had long struck him as true, were even
more applicable than ever. Christ's intention had been to remind
everyone of his hand in creation. As Creator, Christ did not turn
his back to what he had made. He was capable of taking a hand
in all things, and his love, which was boundless, ensured that he
always would. Scoffers, of course, mocked such a notion, as being
little more than flagrant anthropomorphism. To those who did not
have faith, believing such words was the stuff of wish-fulfillment.
Freud, for instance, had in *The Future of an Illusion* hypothesized
that the origin of the idea of God the Father lay in the earliest
stages of psychical development. When a young child was weaned
from the mother's breast, and then in turn came to experience the
pain and fear of realizing that he was not one with the world, but
separate, the newly-emerged world, which stood over and above
the child, appeared threatening and hostile. It was in response
to this infantile terror that the concept of a benevolent heavenly
Father was forged, as a compensation meant to deal with the
trauma. The atheist such as Freud thought that one's needing God
was weakness, and that it suggested faith was a crutch. Yet, this
suspicious interpretation of faith derived its plausibility only by
first tacitly presupposing God's non-existence. After all, a loving

God would want his creation to know and love him. Creating individuals who feel the need to be dependent upon him, thus, was precisely what one should expect to be the case, if the God revealed in Jesus Christ were true. Here, however, was not the place to rehearse all the philosophical and theological reasons he had for dismissing Freud's argument. He felt comfortable in rejecting it, as he long had. When it came to the matter of weakness, recognizing one's need for God led to strength, for in acknowledging one's dependence upon God lay freedom, which of course the natural mind considered to be an oxymoron, since it mistakenly equated obedience to God with repression and oppression.

In any case, what mattered was the clear parallel between the situation described in Matthew's Gospel, and his present one here. Christ had said that if the Father is capable of knowing something as small as a sparrow's fate, will not he take notice of one's own? Elijah smiled peacefully at the thought, realizing that he, like the sparrow, was being watched by God.

"Smiling? The lunatic is smiling!" the woman in the middle sputtered to the man at the window. "Look!"

The man at the window peered over, shook his head incredulously, and put his head back in his hands. Overcome by despair, the man was no longer interested in staring out the window. He had torn off his oxygen mask, and set his life vest on his lap. It was a sardonic, almost rebellious, symbolic gesture, a theatrical action suggesting that if God was ultimately going to allow them to perish, after apparently having initially decided to spare them, he no longer had any interest in pretending there was anything for him to do about it. The man himself, like his vest, was deflated. To that extent, the man's letting-go was akin to faith, since there was no pride of life left in him. He had been forced to admit his dependence on something higher than himself. Yet, there was still something underlyingly spiteful, rather than humble, in it.

"Guess I may as well join you," the man said to Elijah, tossing his vest to the floor. "No point anymore. Who am I kidding? You still praying over there, Moses?"

He understood the man's perspective. Prayer was a mystery. To someone who did not yet trust God, it could appear otiose, even pathetic. He himself had thought about prayer many times. He had even prayed to God to help him better understand prayer itself. It made sense to inquire with God about how to pray properly. After all, Christ had left the Lord's Prayer, as an example of how to pray. Prayer, he had learned in time, was a process always evolving, always deepening, always revealing more—there was never a point at which one knew how to pray perfectly, as if there were no room left to grow. That is what made it wonderful. Always, God had more to teach.

He spoke the familiar words silently in his heart,

"Our Father who art in heaven, hallowed be thy name.

Thy kingdom come, they will be done on earth,
as it is in heaven.

Give us this day our daily bread.

And forgive us our trespasses, as we forgive those
who trespass against us.

And lead us not into temptation, and deliver us
from the evil one.

For thine is the kingdom, and power, and glory,
for ever and ever.

Amen."

When he finished the prayer, his attention returned to what he had been pondering. Strictly philosophically, he knew, this spiritual appraisal of prayer went little ways to answering all the philosophical objections against theodicy. In college, there had been so much talk in his philosophy classes about the infamous 1755 earthquake of Lisbon. He must have heard the story told by a professor at least a half dozen times. A horrific earthquake struck the city, slaughtering many. The atheistic rationalists of the Enlightenment, such as Voltaire, had seized on it, enlisting the calamity as an example of what they saw as clear proof that God does not exist, because if he did, he never would have permitted such an obviously gratuitous evil to occur. Leibniz had made a valiant attempt to account for such events, his metaphysical system of monads maintaining that all things unfolded in accord with a divinely preestablished harmony. According to the German metaphysician, this was, contrary to appearances, indeed the best of all possible worlds. God, who was bound by his nature to actualize only the best of all possible worlds, had elected to create this one, which, *ex hypothesi*, was thus the best.

The aspect of prayer which had interested him was related, but different. Leibniz, and other metaphysicians like him, had felt obliged to explain how free will was possible in the face of what the modern natural sciences had been said to discover, namely that the world was strictly determined. Not long before Leibniz, Spinoza had concluded that the only logical view to draw was fatalism. Human freedom was an illusion. Related to this problem of how to preserve human freedom in light of the world's mechanistic determinism was another problem, that of divine omniscience. For if God already knew everything that would happen before it had, how then were things not fated? Prayers, it would appear, were useless, for they stood no chance of altering the future, which, according even to Leibniz, was foreordained due to divine providence. At the time, he had spent many late nights in his dorm room puzzling over such problems. But there had always seemed to him to be another problem, or better, mystery. It had to do with compossibility. For a world to even be possible, it had to cohere, all the states of affairs must somehow be compatible in order to in turn ever stand the chance of being actualized. The trouble for prayer, then, was one of compossibility. In the world, at any time, many people were praying, and they were all praying for things they wanted, things they wanted to come to pass, things they did not want to come to pass, and so on. There was no possible world in which everyone's prayers could all be answered, since one person's prayer being fulfilled meant the frustration of someone else's prayer. For example, if he prayed that a certain girl he knew in class would fall for him, but one of his friends was doing the same, then there was no possible world in which they both had their prayer answered.

People intuitively registered this point, when they would ridicule the sports fanatic who would pray for his team to win. To pray for such a thing was silly, of course, since the fans of the other team were presumably praying that their own team win as well. How was God to decide whose prayer to answer? It was impossible for God to grant everyone his prayer. Only one team could win. Prayer, then, one might conclude, was a waste of time, for either God's plan was to bring about the state of affairs for which one was praying, or not. If it was part of God's plan, there was no need to pray, for it would come to pass eventually anyhow. And if it was not part of the plan, then no amount of praying would change that. Thus, either way, prayer appeared to be gratuitous.

He found his train of thought, which despite its complexity had been compacted into a few short seconds, interrupted as soon as it had begun. "Hah! The zealot? Of course, he's going to keep praying. Look at him," the woman in the middle whispered resentfully. Before he could say anything in reply, cheers began erupting ahead of them.

"I can't believe it. I can't do this anymore."

"Hah! This is amazing! I'm going to have a heart attack from all this!"

"Thank you! Thank you! Oh, my God, thank you!"

"What is it?" someone a few rows behind the port wing asked. "Tell us!"

A mousey man in a green cardigan, a professor by the looks of it, turned around excitedly, his spectacles flying off his face when his elbow bumped up against the seat behind him, "The engine! It's back on!" As word spread through the cabin, there were cries of elation and incredulous, joyous laughter. The intercom came on.

"Ladies and gentlemen, I, we, well, let's just say we're as exhausted and shocked up here, and, I, well, I don't have the words, really. We know how you all must feel. We feel it too. Somehow, the port engine has just come on again. Nobody has heard of anything like this. It's bizarre. The good news is that we're still in range of Tallahassee. At this point, there's no reason to lie to you. You deserve honesty, as you've all been through enough. The fact is that the fuel is low. It's going to be tight. But I think we can make it. The tower knows we're on the way. We have first priority, obviously. Everyone on the ground is already making preparations for our arrival, and they're going to do everything they can to help guide us in, and take care of you all once we're safely on the ground and finally finished with this." There was a pause. "God sure has a strange sense of humor. I don't mean to offend anyone, but if you feel like it, pray."

Thirteen

H e had already been intending to continue praying before the pilot requested that they all do so. And he wouldn't let the superficiality of the pilot's attitude to prayer dissuade him, either. In life, he had discovered, what others did, and why they did it, was no reason to alter one's own habits and convictions. The situation on the plane was no different. He could feel that the woman and man in the row beside him were speechless, simultaneously euphoric that they once again had dodged death, yet at the same time haunted by what that meant, given the fact that the preceding sequence of events had shattered whatever conception they may previously have held about God's ways. Whereas before they had been ignorant, yet not known it, now they knew they did not know. Registering the full puniness of their own understanding in comparison to God's ways must have been terrifying, so much so, in fact, that neither of them had the strength to conceal their loss for words. There was no more idle chatter, only a telling silence.

If the distance between others and God could be so apparent, he realized that he should take care to make sure he himself had drawn as near as possible to God. Self-examination was never a bad thing.

"Lord, I love you. I want to live. I want to see my wife again. I want to see Sardinia. I want to go back to Anna Lucia and stay in the yellow cottage and feed the manatees. I want to have children one day. I want to show my son how to be a good man, and to follow you. I'm sorry if there is still anything wicked in me. Please, forgive me, for any of my hidden faults. I need your mercy. I need you. Lord, I pray that we survive, so anyone on this plane who is not yet ready to meet you, will have a chance to think about today, and to seek you. Let the plane land in Tallahassee. Let us all learn to fear you, and to not take our lives for granted. Christ Jesus, you are king. I know all things are possible through you. Thank you for your patience with me, for all the years that I was evil, and you showed me mercy. Please tell my wife that I love her, so that if we don't make it, she knows that I was thinking of her, and how much I loved her. Let her rest in you, and know how much you love her."

When his heart had spoken, and he had said enough, it was time to listen. Prayer was not only speaking. It was hearing also.

"Lord, let me hear what you desire me to hear." He cleared his mind, and stilled himself, preparing his heart, so that whatever word he was given might resound within him.

He received an answer, orienting the direction the course his inner life should currently take, in the form of a recollection of natural beauty, not this time of the sea, but of the desert. Or, rather, not so much a desert, but rather a forest oasis within one. Unquestionably, it had been the most beautiful drive he had taken anywhere his whole life, even more beautiful than Big Sur or Carmel. Images of Arizona came to him, and just as earlier it had been as if he were among the eucalyptus, so now it was as if he were there. Next to the narrow highway, a road not unlike the one he would travel to the cove on the Pacific, was a river. He had not been aware of its name, but he had thought it was the Colorado. Passing through the open country, he came across a forest of white aspens, stretching out in both directions as far as his eye could see. He became alert for deer. The road began winding gently, circling downward into a yawning valley, the small town below tucked away amid a forest, not of aspen but pine, the red rock vistas visible in the distance. It had been summer then. He considered pulling over and going for a swim in the river, or renting a tube to travel the rapids. He had even toyed with the idea of renting one of the cabins along the river for a few days. Instead, though, he drove through without stopping, making a promise to himself that one day, as soon as possible, he would return, the next time along with her. Although he was partial to the summer, he knew it would be just as beautiful, perhaps even more so, in the winter after a fresh snow. When they had initially been diving toward destruction here aboard the plane, he hadn't remembered this resolution to someday again visit the desert. Now that he had recollected it, he hoped one day to fulfill it.

The many faces of creation, he realized, the sea and the desert and everything else, were an icon of God's essence, a spectacle displaying the triune God's multitudinous energies, his love, his mercy, his kindness, his grace, his wisdom, his power, his holiness, his faithfulness. Not just natural splendors, but revelations of his secret wonders. If what was manifest now in this world were nothing to be compared with even Eden, it made him ponder what the glory of the kingdom of heaven must be. He could reflect upon nature's variety of beauty indefinitely, and still never come any closer to exhausting its riches. There would always be more he could have recollected, more he could have imagined, more he could have hoped to one day see, or to see again. Something about this inexhaustibility pointed to an even greater infinity, an inexhaustibility of a different degree or magnitude, a beauty of an even higher order. Though it was an excess he could not at all envision, he knew it was the beauty of the Lord.

Fourteen

Beautiful memories of places he had been, or imagined he one day might have gone, ought not be allowed to obscure the experiential fact that sometimes the greatest joys were to be found at home, right among what was the everyday, the routine. To see travel alone as a good was to overlook that the new could be found even in the apparently familiar. It was merely a matter of attitude, of attention. "Give thanks in all circumstances," Paul had told the Thessalonians. What mattered most, ultimately, was gratitude to God, which was Paul's point. But gratitude toward God could be exercised in the appreciation for one's immediate surroundings, regardless of how familiar or otherwise mundane they were, or had become.

It was a lesson he had learned, and would continually seek to reinforce, as the summer nights unfolded at home. He would sit in a plastic chair he had placed on the grass in the back yard. That the chair itself wasn't much, just an item he found when a neighbor had meant to toss it out on garbage day, didn't matter—it being uncomfortable was good, in fact. The reason for sitting outside wasn't to get comfortable in a lavish chair, but to absorb what was all around him. The uncomfortable chair made it easy for him to pay attention, lest he close his eyes and nod off. Dusk would fall, the sky an arctic blue, the whisps of the clouds visible between the roofs of his house and the neighboring house toward the street, the brilliant full moon hovering above the tree line off in the distance behind him. Soon, the lightning bugs would emerge. There would be only a few, and then, in the blink of an eye, they were everywhere. And it was not just they who would awaken then to night. There were the crickets, too, nestled in the grass who announced themselves, and, above them, the cicadas in the trees. He would listen to the latter's night calls, their symphony of small creaturely noises pulsating rhythmically like the beating of a heart. He would tilt back his head, his gaze following the ivy which was wrapping against the trunk of the yard's stoutest tree, the one whose branches hung over the chain link fence separating the neighbor's grass from theirs. He would take off his shoes and socks, gently curling his toes in the grass. The breeze would quicken, he would hear the wind flutter the leaves, which took on the appearance of feathers floating in one place, and he would be reminded of what it had felt like as a boy to play outside on summer nights until the street lights came on and it was time for dinner. Then, amid the stillness, the critters momentarily would pause their song, and there would be a gentle silence, a sweet reminder that he had just been privy to nature's hymnal, its song of praise to the Creator of all things. He would sit contently in that chair, his entire being attuned to the grass yard, which by then felt like a secret garden. Before he knew it, night had consumed the dusk completely, and Ella would open the house door, smile, and put on the porch light, asking him how much longer he would be.

"What're you thinking about out here?"

He smiled. "Just romanticizing the world."

She laughed kindly, "My own little Novalis." She paused. "I love you," she said.

Fifteen

Never in her life had she been so overjoyed yet terrified. To feel both at once so profoundly made the moment the event it was, a unique experience she had never experienced before. Overjoyed because it was finally happening, terrified because it would be such a change. She had always wanted to be a mother, and now she would be, whether she felt ready or not. She was indisputably pregnant. For a number of weeks, she had felt she might be. She had said nothing of it to Elijah. The recent test had confirmed it, and today's ultrasound had revealed another surprise. There were twins, a boy and a girl.

"Congratulations, Mrs. Newman, you are going to be the mother to twins," the doctor said warmly.

She was incredulous. "Twins?"

He saw Ella's anxiety, which he tried to mollify. "We'll do everything we can to ensure the pregnancy goes well, and of course we'll do all we can to ensure a safe delivery. You're in very good health, so a miscarriage is unlikely. Is your husband available?"

"No, he's away right now. Well, actually, he's on his way home. I'm picking him up at the airport in a few hours," she said.

"Fantastic. Please extend my congratulations to him also. He's always welcome to contact us, if he has any questions along the way. And I'll look forward to meeting him, if he decides to accompany you to our next appointment. Cindy at the desk can help you arrange the details," the doctor said. He turned to the nurse. "Sophia, would you walk Mrs. Newman out?"

"Yes, Dr. Richards. This way, Ella," the nurse said happily.

"Thank you, Doctor. This is so wonderful. Terrifying! But wonderful," Ella said.

After booking her next appointment, she got in the car, pulled out her phone, and checked to see if the flight was still due to arrive on time in Atlanta. From the connection, it would be a short flight for Elijah onward to Charlotte. When she opened the application and saw the flight had disappeared from the listings, she worried. It was strange, but she told herself it was probably nothing. She would wait a little while, and if she couldn't find an update online, she'd call the airline.

"I have some good news I need to tell you about when I see you. Love you," she texted.

He would see the message during his layover after he landed in Atlanta. By the time she picked him up in Charlotte, she would be ready to tell him all about what was going on.

"Atlanta," she said to herself. Memories of the downtown skyline summoned images from a year ago, when they had last been in the area. She and Elijah had driven to the island for a week at the beach. On the way home, the car broke down on the highway in downtown. They were forced to pull off to the side and wait. The concrete was sweltering hot, and the rush hour commute traffic whizzing by made her nervous. After calling a tow truck, they had waited hours. At the time, it had felt like such a miserable experience, but she now viewed it with fondness. They had been together, at least. That is what had mattered. Here now, driving home from her doctor's appointment, she felt she would give anything to know that an experience like that would be possible again. When she picked him up later in Charlotte, she would be unperturbed, happy even, she told herself, if they had car trouble on the way home.

Life was fragments, she realized. Some were retained, transfigured by memory. Others faded away forever, the fact that they had been forgotten itself forgotten. She had wanted to take the trip with him to Florida, but work had interfered. Her thought turned to what she knew she had missed. There was the town trolley, of course. She and Elijah would sit at the stop, waiting in the sun, talking about whatever came to mind. Sometimes it would be immediate things, which beach they should go to that day, or what restaurant they might want to eat at later. Other times, they would discuss others, people from her work, old friends, or family. They almost never talked about the world, since the trip was a chance to forget how absurd everything else was. They would talk at the stop, the trolley taking longer to arrive than it should, until it would finally show up, they would board, and take a seat on one of the wooden benches. As they wound their way up main street beside the beach, they viewed the beach cottages, commenting on which they liked, and why.

"Oh, that one is cute."

"Yeah, I like it too," he had said. They couldn't afford it, but maybe one day they would, she had thought. In any case, it was fun to imagine. She would look at the trees and pools and yards, and imagine their kids playing. She knew he was doing the same.

"I still can't believe you don't like Oliver."

He laughed. "Sorry, I just don't."

"It's so cute, though. Oli," she continued.

"That's the problem. It's too cute. It's like you're naming a chia-pet or something," he said laughing.

"Yeah, yeah, I know."

When they would reach the northern point of the island, they would step off the trolley in front of Henry's, a little adobe restaurant with an outdoor patio tucked away beneath the palms. Inside was cozy, the walls of the single-room interior replete with photos of the owner's family and various locals. It was the sort of place that made one feel like one had been eating there for years, even if one were really only visiting. Outside, a man with a guitar would play songs from Hawaii. If it all sounded a little tacky, it wasn't. It was wholesome.

"You want to eat at Henry's tonight?" he had asked.

"Sure, that would be nice."

"You want to take the trolley back to the place after the beach first?"

"Yeah, I'll want to change. I don't mind taking the trolley again back out here. Bean Point. You were right. Most beautiful spot on the island," she had said.

"It reminds me of Hawaii. I guess that's why the restaurant has the guy playing the songs he does."

During the day, on the sand, they would sit next to one another, alternating between swimming in the water and then lounging on the towels.

"I love you," he said.

"I love you," she said. She paused. "I like that about you." She handed him the water.

"Like what?" He handed her the baguette and a slice of orange.

"That you're honest."

"What do you mean?"

"You love me for who I really am, not an image of me."

He blushed.

"What?" she asked.

"Well, that's definitely true. Someone else once mentioned that too."

"Who?" she asked. He was silent for a moment. "The old neighbor? What did she say?"

"It was right after you had dumped me," he said.

"Well, it's true. Most people want someone to love them for who they pretend to be, or wish they were. Which is funny, because most people say they want to be loved for who they really are. But they don't. They just say so."

"Said like a true existentialist," he said.

She laughed. "Existentialist? I don't know. Maybe. An existentialist is just somebody who says aloud what everyone else is really thinking but is pretending not to be."

"Sounds about right," he said.

"But, anyway, the point is that I know you love me for who I am."

"I think you're the same way with me."

She laughed. "That's easy. You're very straightforward. There's no real gap between you and an image. I always liked that about you from the second we met. Me, sometimes I'm not sure who I really am." She paused detecting what others might have thought was a contradiction. "That's what I mean. You love who I really am, even if that means my not fully knowing who I am."

"I know," he said. "Sometimes I'm not sure who I really am. I mean, it's a mystery I think for everyone."

"Isn't that a little bit like God? God always is less than fully comprehensible. It's how he makes us want to seek him. We're made in his image. Strange isn't? The only way to be yourself, to not have an image, is to be faithful to the image of God in us. If we're somehow like him, makes sense that we'd be fathomless," she said.

When he was reading on the beach, she would occasionally look at him, wondering what he was thinking. He put the book down on his lap and turned to her. "What are you thinking about?" he asked.

"Nothing. Just how lucky we are. It's so beautiful here." He was about to say something, but he paused. Instead, he stared out at the ocean and smiled. She wanted to ask him what he was thinking, but she didn't. Here now in the car, thinking about that moment, she wished she had.

"Jude and Emma," she whispered, rubbing her stomach. Well, she would have to ask what he thought, but she felt sure he would agree. So, for now, it was Jude and Emma. She took a deep breath and drove home, images of their future enveloping her with a great peace. "God, help me be a good mother. Please let them not hate me. I'm scared," she said aloud. For a moment, she worried the twins might overhear her, but then she realized that even if they did, they would not understand, and they certainly wouldn't remember. What a mystery it all was.

Sixteen

B ig brown iridescent orbs of fiery passion, flickering with love. Tears of joy were swelling in her eyes, the crystalline flakes from the snow flurry whipping against her porcelain cheeks. Even here, it was as if her face were truly before him, the memory a living memory so powerful that it nearly completely wiped away the ache of her present absence. "Lord God, please let me see her again. Let me see her face, even if it is just one more time. Nevertheless, your will, not mine, be done."

Seventeen

"We have begun our initial descent into Tallahassee. Flight attendants, please make a final check of the cabin." There was cheering, whistling, and clapping from everyone. The pilot, who had paused his transmission expecting the applause, continued, "Ladies and gentlemen, we should have you on the ground in twenty minutes. Local weather is twenty-nine degrees Celsius, eighty-five Fahrenheit, partly cloudy, no winds at the moment." There was another pause, this time for longer. "I, uh, well, I don't really know what else to say. It's been a rollercoaster for us up here, as well. Please stay seated for this last stretch. When we're on the ground, we'll taxi to the gate. We're not exactly sure what the process is going to be, but evidently there may be some additional procedures we'll have to go through before everyone is free to get on with life. Obviously, we'll make the necessary flight arrangements to get you to Atlanta, or wherever your original final destination had been. There will be agents at the gate. Once again, thank you for your patience and courage. For now, sit back, and we'll have you to the gate at Tallahassee shortly."

"I can't wait to get off this thing and to lie down," the man at the window said.

"Don't jinx it," the woman in the middle replied irritably.

"Look, lady, I've put up with you when we were all in bad shape. But, to be honest, I don't have to do that anymore. You really need an attitude adjustment. I don't know whether it was just the stress of the situation or whatever, but please give it a rest."

The woman thought to say something, but thinking it over, she realized the everyday norms of daily life were again in effect. Best to be silent, she decided, and not launch an argument with a man who, in normal circumstances in which the flight had gone as expected, would have remained a total stranger.

The man yawned obnoxiously loudly. "Thanks," he said smugly, seeing that she had chosen to bite her tongue. "It'll be great to get out of here," he said quietly, as if to himself, as he gazed blankly out the window.

Listening to the two's interaction, Elijah wondered what thoughts had been passing through their minds, when the flight had seemed doomed. He wondered if they had prayed, and if so, what they had said to God. He wondered whether they were still considering whatever they may have been thinking when they had appeared destined for death. He wondered whether they intended to forget about it all, or whether they would decide never to forget. He hoped they would not forget, and that they would seek God, but that was not his to decide.

It was Borges, an old college professor of his had once said, who wrote somewhere that one's active knowledge at a given time was determined by the last ten books one had most recently happened to have read. He chuckled quietly recalling the observation, because it explained why, here in the midst of what had just been a near-death emergency, he should find himself somehow of all things suddenly thinking about Solomon Maimon's theory of infinitesimals. It was true, he had discovered, that one's horizons of clear and distinct thought were confined to what one was currently reading, or had very recently finished reading. After completing a book, it would only be a matter of weeks or months before it would be necessary to flip through its pages again, if he wanted to remember what it had said in any detail. Over the years, he had developed the habit of reading more than one book at once, like crop rotation. Not only did cycling through multiple books aid drawing associations and connections among the various ideas, it also helped him sublimate the boredom he would have felt while reading only a single book. Typically, he would read three or four philosophy works at a given time. But always, he would be reading the Bible. A routine had emerged over the years in his spiritual life. He would read from the Scriptures in the morning, most often a selection from the Psalms or Proverbs. And then he would read at night before falling asleep, very often the Psalms again, along with something from one of the Gospels and another New Testament letter. At any given time, he would consequently be reading from both the Old and New Testaments, rotating among the various books and epistles as he felt called and as the exigencies of life demanded. During the day, he would often turn to the Bible, supplementing whatever he was reading of philosophy.

He had been working his way through a book recounting the immediate philosophical reactions to Kant, which explained why Maimon should cross his mind. He had brought the book along to Florida, and he had read most of it while on the beach. Although it was stimulating intellectual history, it was ultimately dissatisfying. Reading all about the intricacies from that period of German philosophical history, of Lessing, Herder, Mendelssohn, Reinhold, Schulze, Hegel, Fichte, and Schelling, reminded him that philosophical systems were quite fascinating. But none of them was true, at least not completely so. One could spend a whole lifetime pouring through the various systems of thought devised over the centuries and never come any closer to the truth, he realized. One would simply immerse oneself in a morass of disagreements and debates. Some people, he knew, claimed to enjoy this. They found the fact that philosophical critique never ended exhilarating. He, too, had once felt this way. But he had come to see it as a purely aesthetic mentality, something indicative of a heart that had not yet resolved itself to committing to the truth of God, and so instead decided to distract itself with the endless complications the various competing philosophical systems afforded. He had sometimes wondered why God gave some people an intellect capable of devising the sort of philosophical systems they did. Probably, he had concluded, such intellect had been a misused gift, something God had intended its recipient to use in order to defend the truth.

As he contemplated his ambivalence over spending time reading the history of philosophy's many systems, the flight attendants began making their way through the cabin. Because the plane now was over land, they said nothing of the fact that he still had not put on his life vest. A few of the others had removed theirs.

"Could you please lower your arm-wrest?" one of the flight attendants asked. She said it smilingly, but it was belied by the pointed exasperation in her tone.

"Oh, yes, sorry," he said.

His mind drifted to Maimon's response to Kant. Kant's famous question in the *Critique* had been how synthetic *a priori* knowledge is possible. According to Maimon, it was impossible to account for such a possibility if one created a dualism between sensibility and understanding as Kant had done. Kant, thus, who thought he had answered Hume's skepticism over causality, by formulating the conditions under which synthetic *a priori* concepts applied to experience, had in fact failed to do so, according to Maimon. Here, Maimon's skepticism entered the picture. For according to Maimon the skeptic, the job of the critical philosopher was not merely to determine the conditions under which synthetic *a priori* knowledge would be possible, but to determine whether or not those conditions in fact obtained. Maimon, ultimately, denied that there was synethic *a priori* knowledge of experience. And yet, at the same time, he resurrected a kind of speculative metaphysics that Kant had aimed to foreclose. For, in order to explain how apparent synthetic *a priori* knowledge was to be explained in terms of analytic knowledge instead, it was necessary, Maimon claimed, to postulate the existence of an infinite understanding. Rather than locating this infinite understanding in the mind of God, as was natural, Maimon instead in effect located it beneath the human finite intellect, within a kind of single universal subject, an *intellectus archetypus*, which creates all the objects in its very act of knowing them. To apply a fitting anachronism from Jung, experiential reality was thus said to be a creation of a great unconsciousness. In addition, everything, including everything that appeared to be contingent, was in fact necessary. This included the deliverances of sense experience, as well all the objects it reveals. Sense perception was said to be little more than confused intellection. Maimon, of course, understood that this all sounded incredibly counterintuitive. So, in order to justify his bizarre conception of reality, he had claimed that what appeared to be contingent about experience only appeared so from the limited finite human understanding. If one were able to sufficiently analyze the nature of experience, however, one would discover that things were the way they were necessarily. Here, it was the famous theory of differentials that came in, since by invoking this piece of theoretical machinery, Maimon believed he was able to explain away the apparent contingency of sensation and that which is encountered in space and time. An infinitesimal was the smallest unit of analysis of sensation. In effect, sensations and all the relations among them were, at bottom, the subconscious production of the infinite understanding, the fabric of the sensible world thereby consisting of an invisible tapestry of differential equations. In Maimon, hence, there was a metaphysics of experience, for the whole of the sensible world was said in principle to be capable of a complete rational explanation.

There was a caveat, of course. For this was the case in principle only—no finite mind could actually ever reconstruct the fabric of reality completely, yet Maimon believed it was nevertheless the philosopher's intellectual duty to strive to do so, even if attaining a perfect comprehension of experience was infeasible. There was something very odd about it all, Elijah mused. Without blushing, the same Enlightenment philosophers who claimed that believing the Bible is the word of God was superstitious or dogmatic could posit the wildest of metaphysical theories. If it were supposed to be a desertion of reason to take the Gospel at face value, how was it not more so to believe that all of experiential reality was a mere appearance or an illusion? There were exceptions to the rule, for there were those who had seen the folly of such systems. The philosopher Hamann, for one, had seen the problem. The Enlightenment notion of a pure reason was an abstract fiction, he had said. And there was also F. H. Jacobi who, for his own part, had argued that secular reason induced nihilism. History, however, had forgotten about both Hamann and Jacobi. They had tried to say in their own ways that the Enlighteners misunderstood what it was to be human, by thinking that the highest calling in life was intellectual inquiry. About that, Jacobi and Hamann were fundamentally correct. The aspiration to submit everything to a conception of pure reason was misplaced. One was not to approach God as a matter of intellectual understanding, but in fear and trembling. Christ was not the God of the philosophers. The point of life was not to develop a theoretical account systematizing human knowing, including the knowledge of God, but to do the will of God, by loving him. As for thinking, it was well and good, so long as it was done in the service of living. But when it was elevated to an end in itself, or treated as if life was not to be lived until thought had first justified it, then one would never live. Dead in one's thought, one would never find eternal life in Christ.

Eighteen

T he experience was itself the souvenir. This he had learned of love and memory. Of course, much of his experience, the majority of it, in fact, had been spent lost without knowing true life, because it had been squandered in a dispersion not knowing the love of God, not knowing Christ. If he were to characterize in what that former life had consisted, he would say now, recollecting it, that it had been a series of failed attempts in love, a futile attempt to find the love of God in anything else, but particularly in romantic loves. Being young and handsome, it had not been difficult to attract women, and, in time, he had become comfortable with doing so. Eventually, he had come no longer to feel guilt or remorse in seducing them. He thought back to the Amtrak surf liner which ran along the Pacific coast. He had ridden the line so many times over the years, which was why it had eventually become a line of broken romances.

His sophomore year of college, there was Isabelle, whom he had met in class. They shared a number of friends from their major. One night at a house party hosted by a mutual friend, she had sat next to him on the couch, making it clear he was her focus. After smoking cigarettes and talking for hours, they exchanged numbers. In the weeks that followed, they saw each other a number of times. But it never stood a chance of lasting. She graduated that summer, and moved home to San Diego for law school in the fall. Bright and ambitious, with an eye to a legal career, she was not the type to be constrained by extraneous responsibilities, which of course meant she eventually would come to the conclusion that it was inconvenient to have a long-distance relationship with a boy still back at college. She invited him to visit her twice that summer. He would take the train. On the way down the coast, he would look out to the sea, chiding himself for wasting his time by coming to see her. He knew he cared more than she did, and soon she would move on.

"This is Elijah," she said to her hometown friends when introducing him at the wharf. "He's—we're seeing each other." It was her way of not lying. She couldn't call him her boyfriend, because obviously there were others. He remembered feeling that he should walk away, head to the train, and never look back. But he stayed.

That weekend had been a huge house party atop a hill overlooking the harbor airport, the jets flying right over the house on their landing approach. Isabelle was inside talking to others, and he had walked out to the yard, where he stood alone among the crowd, watching the city lights below, waiting for the planes to roar from overhead. When they flew over, he would wonder who was aboard, where they were going, and what would become of them in life. At the time, he had felt that it was a moment he would not forget, one he knew was momentous. Maybe it was relishing the sweet sadness of a fleeting youth, or the knowledge that a doomed summer infatuation was coming to an end. But it felt to be more, even if he couldn't express in words what it was that he had been feeling. Only later would he come to conceptualize how that night above the harbor, beneath the procession of planes, had been an initiation into worldly sorrow, a recognition of the subtle decision to attempt to transfigure life into something beautiful through the future memorial of one's present lost choices.

It was possible to be dead while alive, he realized. His thought turned to those lines about the prodigal son. "This brother of yours was dead and is alive again; he was lost and is found."

Isabelle had interrupted his pondering with a tap on the shoulder. She smiled, raising an eyebrow ironically, as if she did not know him. "Hey you, want to get out of here?"

"Sure," he said. "Let's go." They walked through the inside of the house, weaving their way amid the throng of partygoers, and stepped out the front door onto the deserted street.

"A few blocks down the hill, that's where the Casbah is. We should see a show there tomorrow night. Saturday night at the Casbah. Doesn't get better than that."

"You ever been to the Bottom of the Hill?"

"You mean down there? Yeah. All the time. I was at the Casbah last weekend," she said.

"No, I mean the venue. In San Francisco."

"Oh. No, never been." She turned to him, "You'll have to take me sometime."

"Sounds good."

"Rock the Casbah. We're gonna rock the Casbah," she sang laughingly.

They walked slowly, eventually reaching the highway underpass at the bottom of the hill. Isabelle, who had been strolling in the street, hopped drunkenly onto the sidewalk. A second later, an oncoming black sedan sped by them on the underpass curve.

"Wow, that could have been bad," she said roguishly. He wanted to say it was a miracle she had not been killed, but he said nothing. When they got up to her apartment, he had known he was lost. Moreover, he knew she knew that she herself was lost too. She wanted him to embrace it, to enjoy being lost together, but he wasn't yet numb enough to stomach it. It still couldn't sit right with him. She found his residual innocence simultaneously endearing and irritating.

"What's the matter?"

"Nothing," he said, staring out the bedroom window. Usually, he wasn't the sort to lie, but having an honest conversation about them seemed pointless. Headlights flashed across the wall, and they sat in silence, listening to the sounds of the traffic coming from the street below.

When by the end of summer she had stopped calling, he felt heartbroken. For a while afterwards, he thought he had loved her, but eventually he realized maybe he really had just loved the idea of being in love, or of being loved, and not Isabelle herself. She did not truly forget about him, though, he came to learn as the years passed. For a long while, he would periodically get a call from her, asking how he was. Every time, she was drunk. Having thought about the past, she had decided to contact him, evidently indulging in the nostalgic question of what she wondered could have been.

There had been others after her. Rosalind, whom he had known as a young school child, was reintroduced to him by a friend shortly after college. When they saw each other for the first time since childhood, he recognized Rosalind was enamored with the idea that their lives re-entwining must be fate. He could see she was enchanted by the idea of falling in love with him and perhaps marrying, but nothing ever felt right. She was too much of a conformist, he felt. And he drank too much, as far as she was concerned. They were somehow fundamentally different. For one thing, she was Jewish, and her family expected her to marry a Jewish man, which he was not. It was strange, he had thought even then. Rosalind herself was an atheist with no apparent interest in anything but the world. And her family wasn't orthodox. It made him wonder what they thought being Jewish exactly was, and why it should matter. Growing up, her family and others like it had always said that being Jewish was an ethnicity, not a religion. But the root of the former word, *ethnos*, meant a nation or a people. Historically, her family couldn't trace their ancestry to any of the tribes of Israel. Nor did they observe the Torah. And they certainly weren't the spiritual seed of Abraham, the one whom Genesis called the father of faith. For Rosalind, God was an afterthought. As an unbeliever himself at the time, the entire matter had struck him as merely superficial. Yet now, in retrospect, it seemed to him patently absurd. A verse from Romans crossed his mind, summarizing things far better than he ever could, "But he *is* a Jew, which is one inwardly; and circumcision is that of the heart, in the spirit, not in the letter; whose praise is not of men, but of God."

His attention shifted to another trip on the train. He had come from the central coast to the Bay Area to see Rosalind. When the visit was over, in the car, she had kissed him goodbye at the station parking lot before he walked to the platform.

"I have a headache," she said, pressing her hand to her forehead delicately. "Do I have a fever?" He touched her forehead, which was warm and clammy.

"Maybe. I can't tell."

"I'm going to go home and sleep."

When the train pulled out of the station, the parking lot disappearing from view, receding into the unseasonably rainy mist, he had received a text from her. "My headache disappeared. It must have been your kiss." He smiled, encouraged that she wanted to say something meant to assure him that he mattered to her, even if he was taking the train away. That, however, was all it was. Short-lived flattery. Whatever had been between Rosalind and him faded away not long after, as with Isabelle. Things ended with Rosalind and Isabelle, but the quest for what he thought was love continued. During this period of his life, in which there were others to follow, and which stretched on for some years, when he rode the train along the coast, he would step onto the station platform at the stops, light a cigarette and soak up the sun, relishing the fact that he was young. Even then, he had sensed his own foolishness, known that he was romanticizing a form of beauty that was merely fleeting, that he was somehow deeply lost, enamored with the ideality of love, egoistically convinced his sadness would save him.

It was only after meeting Ella that the epiphany occurred. Somewhere along the line, he had become a bad man. A few days after having met her, he returned to California on a trip that had been planned for some time. Being home again meant riding the train along the coast, in order to see all his old friends who were scattered across the state in various cities. At the Salinas stop, he stepped off the train onto the platform to smoke, listening to Bon Iver songs with his headphones on. He checked his phone to find a text from Ella, asking him how the trip was going. He felt a pang of guilt. He loved her already, and he was sure of it. It was entirely different than before with the others. And he felt she perhaps felt differently about him than how the others had. It was then that he realized it. If they were ever to marry and start a family, he would never want their own daughter to fall in love with a man such as

himself. It was not that he was a particularly dishonorable charac-
ter, or that he was deceiving Ella in any way. It was just that deep
down inside he felt lost, and he wouldn't ever want his own daughter depending on a man who felt that way about himself. Contrary
to what the youthful pride of life had led him to believe up to then,
he knew at once he was not magnificent. When he thought further
about it on that platform in the sun, he recognized the only truly
good man was the one whom loved God.

Words he had been suppressing for years entered his mind.
This time, he could not ignore them. "He who finds his life shall
lose it, but he who loses his life for my sake shall find it." If he truly
was to love Ella, he would have to seek God, so that he could be
worthy of the love, and hope, she had for him. Standing on the
platform, he had put out the cigarette, walked to his seat in the
passenger compartment, and then stared out the window as the
train left the station. In a way he could not articulate, the endless
miles of strawberry fields and oak hills somehow spoke to him,
admonishing him for how much of youth he had frittered away on
false love, on a train line to nowhere.

The afternoon sun shone harshly through the wide compartment window. He put on his black sunglasses, took a long sip of
his lukewarm coffee, and closed his eyes. Something, he knew, had
changed. With Isabelle or Rosalind or the others, he had thought
about how one day, long after they no longer knew one another, she
would think of him, periodically recalling some moment between
them. Her memory, and his minor place within it, was a form of
eternity. Yet, only a form. For the ideality of what they had experienced together, along with her image of him from the past, would
cease to be once she died, assuming death really was indeed the end.
But with Ella, it was all different. He didn't feel himself striving to
have an experience merely fated to be recalled later, long after they
had parted. He didn't want to part. He didn't desire to be a future
memory of hers. He wanted to be with her forever.

Here aboard the plane, he was grateful to God to know that he
had changed since that train, that he had tried to make the most of
the time he had thus far been given with Ella. The fact that the love

had been true, not squandered, would make it all the sadder when it finally did come to an end. But for now, he felt grateful knowing he was nearly home, and there would be more.

Nineteen

T hinking about the ornate metaphysical yarns of the philosophers brought to mind a verse from the Old Testament. It was in Ecclesiastes, he was sure, although he flipped to the page anyway just to see it.

> God has made man upright, but they have sought out many inventions.

It seemed to him that perhaps the biggest invention of all was a theological one, the myth of the doctrine of total depravity. He had contemplated that piece of theological dogma many times, only to find it wanting. He was not alone. For centuries, none of the early church fathers had ever suggested man was born with a sin nature as a consequence of the Fall. The consequence of the Fall had been mortality, not depravity. The latter notion had arisen with Jerome first, then later to be popularized by Augustine. Augustine calculatedly destroyed his adversary, Pelagius. In short order, what had been considered orthodoxy was declared heresy, and for centuries ever since, all the churches, including the Protestant denominations, had been propagating the doctrine of man's depravity. Luther had done so most famously, as had Calvin. Yet these theologians had turned the truth on its head. Rather than acknowledging man was made in the image of God, and thus free to obey God, they had invented systems claiming that man was born in a state of corruption, one thereby inhibiting, or even outright disabling, the ability to obey God. Some of these systems, including Calvin's own, had contended that God through an eternal decree before creation had chosen who would be saved, and who would be damned. Everyone was born a sinner, so the thought went, yet not everyone would be a recipient of God's mercy. That was the predestination part. He could see why the woman in the middle next to him rightly scoffed at such notions. She was correct to reject them. Those who embraced the idea of congenital depravity did so, he assumed, because it gave them an excuse for their sin, as they could always take solace in the purported fact that they were constitutionally incapable of being good. Theology gave license to rationalize evil as a birth defect. Many people, it seemed to him, never went further than either rejecting or accepting this idol of a predestinarian God. Whereas the former were atheists estranged from the true and living God, the latter believed they knew God, but they did not, for they were actually worshiping a false image of God. From what he had seen, the woman in the middle was one of these atheists, the man at the window one of these false believers.

"A good man out of the good treasure of his heart brings forth good things, and an evil man out of the evil treasure brings forth evil things."

This is where death came in, Elijah saw. When evil entered creation, the only way to overcome it, by purging it, was by giving each man a finite allotment of days. The reason for this choice by God, Elijah inferred, was that God knew everyone would invariably succumb to temptation, and many would in turn come to enjoy a life of sin. If such types were never to die, they would continue happily on in their evil, since they would have no incentive to abandon their course and follow good instead. Foreseeing this, God had elected to introduce death as a warning. Death was a reminder to everyone that no matter how much one enjoyed evil or living for oneself in the world, it must eventually come to an end. Death, thus, was a reminder of the inevitable judgment of God and that the world was passing away. It was also, Elijah saw, God's way of separating those who were willing to love him from those unwilling to do so. When one saw that life on earth was finite, one had a choice—either to serve God for the rest of one's days, or not. Those who chose the latter course were not fit for God's kingdom, because they did not want to be part of it. This, Elijah thought, was the mistake of the woman in the middle. She believed that God was arbitrarily barring some from heaven while

letting others in. Yet, really, nobody was excluded from the kingdom of heaven but those in life who hadn't wanted to be included.
A stretch of text entered his consciousness encapsulating his preceding line of thought. It was memorized, so he simply ruminated
on it without turning over to the physical passage.

> "For none of us lives to himself, and no one dies to himself.
>
> For if we live, we live to the Lord; and if we die, we die
> to the Lord. Therefore, whether we live or die, we are the
> Lord's.
>
> For to this end Christ died and rose and lived again, that
> He might be Lord of both the dead and the living."

These words of Paul induced a deep serenity in him. Worry-
ing could not add even a single hour to his life. But prayer, which
was the other of worry, could move a mountain. Much better,
then, to pray than to worry. The lifeblood of existence was not
thinking, but prayer. This was why, he presumed, the Bible stated
that one was to pray without ceasing. He cleared his mind, so that
he could hear the words of Christ speak.

"Peace I leave with you, my peace I give to you; not as the
world gives do I give to you. Let not your heart be troubled, neither
let it be afraid."

"Let not your heart be troubled; you believe in God, believe
also in me. In my Father's house are many mansions; if it were not
so, I would have told you. I go to prepare a place for you. And if I
go and prepare a place for you, I will come again and receive you
to myself; that where I am, there you may be also."

Elijah's heart was still for a moment, and then replied, "Lord,
I love you. Thank you for your strength. Let me be with you. Let
everyone seek your face. Let the face of my heart face yours."

Twenty

"Till we meet again." It was a commonplace phrase, something many said in the wake of the death of a loved one. But it was also an expression at which others scoffed. There was the argument, again popularized by Freud, that the hope of immortality was a childish wish, an illusory desire, insofar as it was based on false hope, rather than substantive evidence. People believed it, not because they were convinced it was true, but because it provided them comfort. It lessened death's sting. So went the argument, anyway. The thing that had long interested him, however, was not so much the atheistic argument against the hope of immortality, but that many of those who mocked the notion of life after death for its supposed lack of evidence, would simultaneously assert that they knew there was no afterlife. Death was it. Or, so they claimed. But how were they in any position to know? If death were the ultimate mystery of life, and nobody could know what it entailed until one had died, how could those who dismissed the idea that it was possible to see one another again in the next life know that there was no such life. They had not yet died. For all they knew, then, death was not the end. The only conclusion Elijah had been able to draw from this was that those who denied the hope of immortality must not desire it. They rejected the hope of immortality, declaring it a delusion, because they desired that death be the end of their whole existence. There was something very monstrous about that mentality, he had always felt. The origin of atheism was not strictly intellectual, then. It went deeper. Having ruminated on it over the years, Elijah believed he had reconstructed the process by which one ended up this way. First, at some point in life, one fell headlong into sin and enjoyed it. Then eventually, one's guilty conscience became too much to ignore, and the fear of divine judgment overtook one. Consequently, it was necessary to convince oneself that God did not exist, and when one had done so, one was free to return to the dissolution one had been previously enjoying, as there was once again no fear of judgment. Better not to believe there is a God, than to believe one was on the road to perdition. That was the psychological maxim of those who refused to repent. It was wishful thinking lying behind atheism and the denial of immortality, then. Although this was a view that he had arrived at on his own by reflecting on what he had seen of others in life, he was apparently in good company. Recently, he had discovered the Cambridge Platonists had once all held such a view also. He had nearly decided to take a book about them on the trip, but he had packed the book about the post-Kantians instead.

The train of thought did not end there. Thinking more about it, people who lived so were invariably plagued by depression, anxiety, substance abuse, among other demons. They were unhappy, which was interesting, given that they had expressly made their life all about the pursuit of happiness, rather than eternal happiness. They did this, because not to do so would be to lie to oneself. This is what they said, anyway. They said they were atheists who denied immortality because to believe anything otherwise was wishful thinking. Elijah's thought shifted to the matter of depression and pharmacology. People everywhere were on anti-depressants, looking for relief from their anxiety and depression. The medical industry, and culture as a whole, held that depression was caused by a chemical imbalance, a purely physiological ailment that could be alleviated by biochemical means. Such a notion of the origin of depression went all the way back to Oxford's Robert Burton's *The Anatomy of Melancholy*, the early seventeenth-century text which had claimed depression, or melancholy, was a humor attributable to excess bile in the brain. There was an unintended richness in this modern consensus that moods, including depression, were effectively manipulable by psychotropic medications. Such a consensus was assumed to be scientific, rational, and enlightened. But the Greek root behind the terms pharmacy and pharmacology was *pharmakeia*, which meant sorcery, the use of administering drugs, often for magical arts, as a form of idolatry. Ancient sorcery, or magic, had been the attempt to harness supernatural forces to control and manipulate physical reality. The modern psychiatric industry was a kind of carnal superstition. Harnessing the powers of drugs, it aimed to exorcise reality of anything supernatural, by denying the existence of forces above and beyond the merely physiological. Yet, by doing so, the endeavor lapsed into a form of superstition itself, with lost, miserable people being told to pop happy pills that were supposedly capable of delivering them from their despair. In the name of deferring to what modern psychology deemed a natural explanation of the phenomenon, the public had come to believe, without evidence, that depression was caused by a chemical imbalance of the brain. When this theory was disproven for lack of evidence, rather than admit the very belief that the supernatural could be banished was the myth, those who had gullibly succumbed to the first failed reductionistic explanation of depression would flock to the next one on offer. Elijah chuckled to himself. The Enlightenment definition of dogmatism was holding a belief on the basis of deference to authority, to trust without sufficient reason. It was odd, he thought, how most atheists chose to trust what they did. They were worldly dogmatists, placing their unflagging confidence in society's institutions, no matter how corrupt, dishonest, irrational, and unreliable those systems proved to be.

There was no reason to dwell further on the absurdities of the modern reductionist conception of the human being. All that mattered, he decided, was the fact that to invoke the supposed authority of atheist Enlighteners, as if their philosophies had shown that there was no immortality, was dishonest. Kant, for one, had argued that immortality was neither verifiable nor falsifiable. To presume to know immortality was not in the cards was specious knowledge. Even more to the point, Elijah thought, was the example of Socrates. Socrates had entertained the notion of death's potentially being a blessing. The just individual, said Socrates, should look forward to death, since it very well could mean that one would depart to a better place than here. What it came down to was that those who were unjust in this earthly life feared judgment, so they told themselves that death would be their extinction. Just as the hope of immortality reflected the desire of the just to continue being, so too the rejection of such hope reflected the desire of the unjust to cease living, to not be accountable for how they had lived.

His mind turned to Acts. In one chapter, he was pretty sure it was seventeen, the famous chapter in which Paul confronted the Greek philosophers in Athens, it was explained that God had raised Jesus from the grave to demonstrate that bodily demise was not the end of existence, and that there was a judgment to come. The rejection of Christ, along with his teachings and the testimony of his life, including the event of the resurrection, must ultimately be rooted in the fact that the reality of bodily resurrection was an unacceptable prospect for those who did not yet love God and were not living as God commanded. Denial of immortality was the deepest act of rebellion of which a person was capable, he saw. It was foolish to think anyone could know that there was nothing after death. And it was foolish to claim that the evidence suggested there was nothing to follow it. In the wake of the resurrection, all the evidence showed otherwise. There was eternal life, if only one would simply seek it. How strange, he thought, it must be to be someone who lived a whole lifetime not wanting to be raised from the dead, and would rather remain dead forever, if only one could. The idea of a Lazarus who would prefer never to be raised—how sad, he thought. The atheistic denial of immortality was the death-drive *par excellence*. God had offered man eternal life, yet many preferred instead to live in the shadow of death, living strictly temporal existences that suppressed the knowledge of God, and hence eternity.

Other words of Paul, this time from Romans, stirred within him, "When they knew God, they glorified him not, but became vain in their vain imaginations, and their foolish heart was darkened. Professing themselves to be wise, they became fools."

He glanced out the window across the aisle, when he heard the flaps being extended. In a few moments, the landing gear would be lowered, and they would be on the ground. As he contemplated everything that had transpired, a psalm of David entered his mind, "When will I appear before God?" He had been prepared for death, at least as much as one could be, and yet now it had fled. He was grateful for all the gifts of this life, gifts he would be able to enjoy once again. "Lord God, thank you. Thank you for your mercy. Please let me be worthy of your loving kindness. I love you." He took out his phone from his bag. Ella had said that she would be busy around the time he was originally due to land. She might not answer, but he would call her from Tallahassee, to at least leave a message.

Twenty-One

H e had not replied. That was very unlike him. He always replied to texts. Even more disconcerting was the fact that the
Atlanta flight was not yet updated on the online tracker. She considered calling the airline, but as she was only a few minutes from
home, she decided she could wait and call from there. Better not to
risk an accident on the highway, she thought.

* * *

She merged into the slow lane from the ramp. It was then that she
felt her heart pierced, her body filled with a dread she had not
imagined possible. In a flash, a part of herself was gone, and although she had been trying to tell herself ever since leaving the
doctor's appointment that the uneasiness she was feeling was
probably nothing, there was no longer any denying it.

* * *

Three miles out from the runway, the pilot had engaged the landing gear. Or, rather, the pilot had attempted to do so. For reasons
that would occupy the investigators for months to come, the
landing gear somehow jammed, and did not deploy. The plane
would have to land on its belly, and everyone aboard would simply have to hope for the best. Back in the cabin, the passengers
and flight attendants had only moments to process what they
were being told. The intercom came on again.

"Something's wrong! Everyone, brace for impact!"

Elijah opened his phone hurriedly, to send a text he was un-
sure would ever reach her. "You'll hear about it on the news. Engines went out. Out of fuel. Then landing gear. I love you so much.

You are my soulmate. Please don't ever give up. Christ loves you. I will see you in the kingdom."

A few rows ahead, the family from before was again disconsolate. The husband was staring into space, inattentive to anything around him, including his wife and daughter. The mother, who had previously been violently upset, was now sitting silently with tears streaming down her face. The young girl was tugging on the mother's shirt, trying to get her mother's attention.

"Mommie! Mommie! What's wrong? Look at me! Look!" The girl had put a doll on her mother's lap, but the mother did nothing.

"Mommie?"

The mother came out of her trance momentarily, looked at her daughter, and smiled feebly. "I love you," the mother said.

"I love you too, Mama," the girl said happily, oblivious to the danger. "What's wrong?"

"Nothing," the mother said. The girl removed her seat belt and began to squirm out of her seat.

"No, no," the father said, securing her seatbelt.

"But I want to go. I need to go," the girl said.

The father lied. "We'll go in a minute. Just wait for now," he said.

Watching the family began stirring images of Ella and children of their own. He involuntarily wondered how he would handle such a situation, if they had been here, but there was no way to know, since he was alone. When he tried to picture it, his imagination failed. It was too painful to think about, so he let the inchoate apparitions dissolve, as he strained to turn his attention to something else.

* * *

The red sun sunk below the city, stretching a purple shadow across the valley. A violent wind was tearing through the soldiers' encampment on the hill. He saw the Son of man lift his head to heaven and cry. "It is finished! Father, into thy hands I commend my spirit."

* * *

A man and woman lied together nude in the shaded glade, the thunderous roar of the nearby rushing river concealing the words they exchanged. He saw the serpent slithering toward them, and he wondered what he would have done had he been the first man.

* * *

Big brown iridescent orbs of fiery passion, flickering with love. But these were tears of grief streaming from her eyes, and there was no way he would be able to wipe them away.

* * *

Seated at the tavern with a group of friends, a man entered and gazed at him fixedly. The man raised a finger, pointing. The others at the table looked to see how he would respond. He wondered, if he had been Matthew, called at the seat of custom, whether he would have stood to follow. He felt like he had done what he could to follow in this life. "Mercy, oh God."

* * *

In those final seconds while still aloft, everyone aboard was as silent as a stone. As for Elijah, he was as stunned as everyone else. He did what he could to compose himself. He would not dwell on what was not to be, but instead make his last train of thought one of praise.

"Lord, I am sorry for everyone I have harmed, anyone I have wronged, anybody I have hurt. Please let them heal, let them find peace and joy and life in you."

He pictured her, "I will miss you."

"Christ Jesus, please tell her that I love her. Let her know I regret having taken everything for granted."

"I brought nothing into the world. I carry nothing out."

"The Lord giveth and the Lord taketh away, blessed be your name."

"I know that I was nothing. Take me."

Twenty-Two

A way to die as horrifying as it is captivating, a plane crash compels the public's fascination, and is what the world considers to be a newsworthy event. This particular crash was sure to be no exception, and so this event that claimed the lives it did would be mentioned far and wide, albeit only briefly. When the stories of it broke later that evening on television and then in the papers the next morning, the basics would be recounted. None of what would be said, however, would reveal the essential. There would be speculation concerning the potential cause of the crash, the identities of some of those who had perished would be noted solemnly, there would be statements from government flight officials and airline representatives assuring the public that what had happened was rare and would be thoroughly investigated, and of course, comments from the loved ones of those who were gone would be issued as well. All of this chatter was for the world, a world for which death remained a public spectacle to be treated as an item of curiosity, as an event that had in this instance afflicted these others, but would one day, in one way or other, befall everyone else also. The news coverage would be accordingly impersonal, a fleeting distraction for those who, watching or reading of it, would themselves simply be relieved not to have been one of the unlucky others on the plane to have died. In short, nobody who learned of the crash on the news would penetrate what about it was most remarkable, and what would have been most worthy of reporting, were it possible to do so, which it was not. Nothing on the news would penetrate the mystery of death, or of the fate of those who had died on the flight. Nor, then, would those who heard about it on the news understand why it was wrong to conclude, as they did, that the crash had been a misfortune for all involved.

The pilot responsible for the miracle maneuver was imme-diately heralded as a hero. "I don't know what to say," he would tell the reporters. "You could run that scenario a thousand times, and every single time but this one, we'd have all died. I did what I could, but it was out of my control." The copilot was seriously injured, and would require months of physical rehabilitation. His flying days were likely over. Yet, he was alive.

Many of the passengers were severely injured. There were those horrendously burned, others with various parts of their bodies mangled or crushed. Some would require amputations. But again, they had survived. There was the young tattooed man, among them. Seated a few rows behind the wing, he had caught a large piece of shrapnel from the engine turbine, his hand and lower arm shredded to ribbons as a result. The surgeons would elect to amputate below the elbow. Aside from being alive, how-ever, there was the further fact, one the man himself took to be a sign of divine providence, that because the damage to his arm had been relegated to where it was, his largest, most ornate tattoo, a tribal pattern on the bicep, had been spared. The family with the redheaded mother and toddler were completely unscathed, except of course for the slap mark on the child's cheek, which the mother regretted having given her, and everyone pretended not to notice. The woman in the middle seat and the man at the win-dow had both survived, even if they were battered and bruised. The woman had suffered a concussion, broken a number of bones, and lost her front teeth when her head hit the seat in front of her. It was impossible to say how the event would precisely change her, but a change was certain. As for the man, he would be partially deaf after the ear facing the window was torn off from flying metal debris. Aside from that, he was fine. So, too, was the professor in the cardigan, who, though he knew the public would classify what he had survived as a miracle, remained reluctant to categorize it as such. "Inexplicable good luck," he would say, whenever he tried explaining it to others in the years to come, beginning with the news reporters that evening.

As expected, there were fatalities. The two flight attendants seated in the chairs up front had perished, the particular section of the plane in which they had been seated evidently being the least capable of absorbing the shock of impact. Their necks, the coroner would find, were snapped. The third flight attendant, the one who had fainted in the aisle after the starboard engine had exploded, survived, suffering nothing more than a series of ugly lacerations on her arm requiring extensive stitches.

Of the ninety passengers, only eight had died. It was truly extraordinary, considering that in an emergency landing such as the one performed, it would have been virtually impossible for anyone to survive had the crash unfolded as it almost certainly should have. Among the few dead were the six passengers who had been seated directly at the wings. When the wings tore loose, their shards ripped to pieces those immediately near the resulting holes in the fuselage. Additionally, there had been another man, who, seated fairly well behind the wing sections, had died from blunt force trauma, though the precise cause of the extensive injuries to his head would never be fully determined. As it happened, the man was the same man who had helped the young flight attendant to her feet. And finally, there was the one whom the woman from the middle seat and the man at the window would simply remember as the man from the aisle seat, Elijah.

Ella had been watching the news coverage on the television when her phone rang.

"Mrs. Newman?"

"Yes."

"Hi, Ella. This is Arthur Naples with the airline. Do you have a moment?"

"Yes," she said, her voice quivering.

"I'm calling—well, as I'm sure you know, there has been an incident. The flight to Atlanta that your husband was on crashed in Tallahassee. We're not sure what exactly happened, but we are going to get to the bottom of it, I promise."

"I don't really care—"

The man cleared his throat and interrupted. "I'm sorry. I don't mean to imply that what caused the accident is what matters. I'm calling obviously to give you an update on the information we have regarding the passengers." There was a pause.

"Yes?"

"Well, it's something of a, well, it's a miracle really. The plane, which was on fumes, made an emergency landing without the landing gear down. Everyone should be dead. But our preliminary reports are that there are many survivors."

"Is he okay?" she asked, knowing that if he were, the man at the airline would have already said so.

"I—we don't know. We're still sorting that out. Some persons are as yet unaccounted for." That meant Elijah was among them. Those who had survived had already contacted their loved ones. Those who were too injured and in no state to do so themselves would have had their loved ones contacted by the airline. She would not hear from anyone, including the airline, until they had found his remains and confirmed the death. She began sobbing.

"Please, please—I'm sorry. Don't cry. We're hopeful that there could still be more. I will be in touch. If there is anything at all we can do, please don't hesitate to contact us." An awkward silence lingered over them for a few seconds.

"Thank you," she said, fighting through the tears.

"You're welcome, Mrs. Newman." The phone clicked off.

Alone in the house, she stared at the television numbly. It was all so grotesque. She felt violated, as if everyone who had no right to do so were intruding. Of course, she herself had watched news coverage of other calamities. When she had done so, she always thought about how those personally affected by what she was seeing must be hurting unimaginably, and must feel dehumanized by the fact that others such as herself were looking on. This strange impersonal fascination with death, a fascination that turned it into a spectacle, was monstrous. In a way, watching a television report of the death of others was no less tasteless than gawking at a car wreck on the roadway.

Ella unmuted the television coverage. A young blonde reporter named Jennifer Taylor, dressed in a black miniskirt and white high heels, was standing on the terminal curb at the airport. As she began speaking, the station telecasted images of the crash scene live, showing the flashing lights of the fire engines and ambulances.

"Hi, Tammy. At 6:34 PM this evening, a plane carrying ninety passengers from Sarasota made an emergency landing at the Tallahassee International Airport here behind me." The screen showed a map of the southeast, with a red line drawn of the flight path from Sarasota to Atlanta.

"The flight, which we know had originally been intended for Atlanta, was diverted after experiencing trouble with an engine." The line shifted, this time terminating in Tallahassee. A small icon of an airplane was placed on the map showing where the emergency had begun.

The coverage cut to Jennifer, who was brushing her hair off her face from a gust of wind, as she tried to continue reading from her notepad. "The details are not yet clear, but after having spoken to some of those close to the situation, the initial engine problem happened over the Gulf of Mexico, we've been told. The pilot, Christopher Arceneaux, diverted the plane's course to land. It was while on route here that the second engine failed." A photo of the pilot appeared on the screen, then a small icon of the plane was added to the map graphic, this time where the second engine failure had taken place.

"That was when everyone aboard thought they would die. Somehow, one of the engines came back on. Everyone aboard we've spoken to said it was a miracle. And yet, it was not to be. Right before landing, something went wrong again. This time the problem was not with the engines. Instead, the landing gear failed." A computer graphic of the airplane came on the screen. A simulation began, the plane's two engines shown on fire, the landing gear failing, and then the plane scraping against the runway.

"Just moments before having to attempt a belly landing, the pilot informed everyone aboard. They braced for impact, assuming they would all die." The coverage showed stock images of commercial airliners landing. A live shot of the scene from a helicopter appeared.

"Somehow, Tammy, tonight many of those passengers can say they're alive. It really is something. We'll have more on what happened when we've had a chance to interview the pilot, Christopher Arceneaux. And we hope to air interviews with a number of the passengers that we've talked to." The anchor in the studio appeared on a split screen.

"Jennifer, harrowing story. Everyone's worst fear when they fly. We're so lucky that tonight we can report that things aren't much worse than they could have been. When we return, we'll have additional live coverage of this developing story. We're expecting to hear from officials about the crash shortly. The FAA and NTSB will be holding a press conference. Again, if you're just tuning in, there's been a crash at the Tallahassee International Airport. We'll have more soon." A mattress commercial came on.

Twenty-Three

E lla switched off the news and walked out the door, where she stood on the porch, listening to the crickets, while looking up at the pink and blue sky. She wiped away the tears trickling down her cheeks, sighed gently, then smiled softly. He was gone, but not forever, for she knew he must have died faithfully, knowing too, as she did, they would see one another again in the life to come. She was about to head inside, when she saw the plastic chair in the yard, the old thinking chair Elijah loved—had used to love. She walked down the porch steps and took a seat on the grass. She had no desire to be false, which was why she admitted to herself, and to God, that she wished she could die now too. The pain of knowing he was gone felt to be too much to bear.

The phone vibrated, and she looked to find a text. A message from Elijah! She jumped from the grass and walked over to the steps, where she took a seat, frantic and elated at the thought that he was here, and read hungrily. She fell to her knees in grief when she finished. They would never see the coast of Sardinia together. There would never be a family beach cottage in Anna Lucia next to Bob and Clara. They would never again feed the manatees lettuce. They would never tube down the river and walk among the desert pines. They would never sit atop the sea bluffs, taking in the smell of the eucalyptus. Everything was reduced to an all-encompassing *never*. He really was gone.

"Oh, that I had wings like a dove! for then would I fly away, and be at rest. Lo, then would I wander far off, and remain in the wilderness," her heart uttered. More tears fell. "You will see him one day in heaven," she whispered to Jude and Emma.

* * *

Shortly before Ella was to sit outside in the chair that night thinking of him among the lightning bugs and crickets, Elijah had experienced precisely what she knew to be so, but the world did not.
He had perished, but not eternally.

The two passengers from the aisle, the man at the window
and the woman in the middle, were unable to recall for investigators what exactly had happened during the crash, other than that
they discovered his body lifeless next to them once the plane had
come to a stop, and they had checked on him. They did not know
it, but Elijah's spirit had left the plane just a split second after
impact, well before the fiery wreckage had finally come to a rest
at the end of the runway.

Death, he had found, really was a chariot of fire. After dying,
which had proved to be a crossing rather than an end, he was
taken up, to where he was greeted by the words promised to him,
"Well done good and faithful servant." The glory of the voice wel-
coming him from on high was alone sufficient to bring down the
flood of joyful tears it did, to say nothing of the heavenly host of
angels, whose song was too beautiful for the world he had just
departed to contain.

* * *

She knew she had never read it as often as she should have. The
Bible had always intimidated her. And as much as she loved God,
and knew God loved her, a guilt she had known since childhood
would still sometimes haunt her. If she were honest, it was difficult
to accept God truly could love her. She had felt unworthy, which
was why it was so wonderous to comprehend that God's love was a
superabundance, something that was accessible, even if one hadn't
merited it. That was the love of Christ, she thought. Words she had
not pondered in some time unexpectedly welled up within her,
comforting her, for now she understood.

> "And God shall wipe away all tears from their eyes; and
> there shall be no more death, neither sorrow, nor crying,

82

neither shall there be any more pain: for the former things are passed away.

Then He who sat on the throne said, Behold, I make all things new. And He said to me, Write, for these words are true and faithful.

And He said to me, It is done! I am the Alpha and the Omega, the Beginning and the End. I will give of the fountain of the water of life freely to him who thirsts."

At the threshold, she turned around to view the empty chair in the yard one more time before going in. When she opened the door to come inside, she kept the porch light on outside.

"Till we meet again," she said tenderly.